D0193490

This book belongs to

How many **Fairy Animals** books have you collected?

- 🌼 Chloe the Kitten
- 🌼 Bella the Bunny
- 🌼 Paddy the Puppy
- 🌼 Mia the Mouse
- 🌼 Poppy the Pony
- 🌼 Hailey the Hedgehog

And there are more magical adventures coming very soon!

Fairy Animals
of misty Wood

Mia the Mouse

Lily Small

Henry Holt and Company
New York

With special thanks to Thea Bennett

Henry Holt and Company
Publishers since 1866
175 Fifth Avenue
New York, New York 10010
mackids.com

First published in the United States in 2015 by Henry Holt and Company.
Originally published in Great Britain in 2013
by Egmont UK Limited.

Library of Congress Cataloging-in-Publication Data
Small, Lily.
Mia the mouse / Lily Small. — First American edition.
pages cm. — (Fairy animals of Misty Wood ; 4)
"Originally published in Great Britain in 2013 by Egmont UK Limited."
Summary: Mia is in the middle of telling a story to her sick grandmother when her mother
asks her to run an errand, but, distracted by what may come next in the story, all Mia can
remember is that she is to fetch something that starts with "B." Includes activities.
Paper Over Board ISBN 978-1-250-11398-6 — Paperback ISBN 978-1-250-11399-3
[1. Fairies—Fiction. 2. Mice—Fiction. 3. Storytelling—Fiction. 4. Bees—Fiction.] I. Title.
PZ7.S6385Mi 2015   [Fic]—dc23   2014047285

Henry Holt books may be purchased for business or promotional use.
For information on bulk purchases, please contact the Macmillan Corporate
and Premium Sales Department at (800) 221-7945 x5442 or by e-mail
at specialmarkets@macmillan.com.

First American Edition—2015
Printed in the United States of America by LSC Communications,
Harrisonburg, Virginia

Hardcover
1 3 5 7 9 10 8 6 4 2

Paperback
5 7 9 10 8 6 4

Contents

CHAPTER ONE

A Good Little Mouse

Deep in the Heart of Misty Wood,
there was an oak tree so tall its
branches seemed to touch the
sky. Its leaves were as green as

emeralds, and they loved to dance in the breeze. The oak tree's thick, knobby roots stretched deep into the soil and held the tree steady.

If you looked carefully, in between the tree roots, behind a cluster of tall green ferns, you would see a hole leading down to a cozy burrow. And if you looked very carefully indeed, you would see a little mouse sitting on the grass next to the hole. The mouse's

name was Mia, and she lived in
the burrow with her mom and dad,
her grandma, and her four baby
brothers and sisters.

Mia was a Moss Mouse—one
of the fairy animals of Misty Wood.
Her beautiful fairy wings were

transparent, just like a dragonfly's, and when the sunshine touched them, they twinkled violet and green. Her fur was as golden as honey— except on her tummy, where it was snow white—and she had long, silky whiskers that wiggled and twirled whenever she was excited.

Mia was making a cushion from a ball of soft green moss.

"Pat-a-cake, pat-a-cake, pat-a-cake!" she sang to herself as she

rolled the moss along the ground and patted it into a nice round shape with her tiny pink paws.

Just like all the fairy animals of Misty Wood, the Moss Mice had a special job to do to make the wood a wonderful place to live. The mice made soft, squishy cushions out of moss and placed them all around the wood so the other fairy animals would have somewhere comfortable to sit.

"Pat, pat, pat!" Mia sang as she shaped the cushion.

"Hello, Mia!" a voice called.

There was a scrabbling noise from inside the hole, and a face with bright beady eyes and long silvery whiskers popped out. It was Mia's dad.

"I'm afraid Grandma's come down with a nasty case of the sniffles," he said. "Will you go and keep her company? Mom's busy

with the babies, and I've got to go out and collect some more moss for our cushions."

"Of course I will," Mia said.

Mia's dad gave her a twinkly-eyed smile. "You *are* a good little mouse! Perhaps you could tell Grandma one of your stories. I bet she would appreciate it." And with that, he jumped out of the hole, twirled his whiskers, and unfurled his wings. They glinted silver in

the sun. "See you at teatime!" Mia's dad called as he flew off through the trees. He carried a big bag made from spider silk in his front paws.

Mia picked up her cushion and hurried underground. The passageway to the burrow was nice and cool and smelled of fresh earth. Mia's whiskers began to twitch. Telling stories was her favorite thing in the whole wide world. She loved it even more than making cushions.

Mia scampered into the burrow. At one end, her mom was busy feeding the babies. At the other, Grandma was tucked into her bed of soft moss.

Mia hopped over to her. Grandma was curled up in the middle of the bed with her nose peeping over the edge. Normally, Grandma's nose was pale pink, but today it was red. Mia got a little closer. Normally, Grandma's black

eyes shone and there was a happy
smile on her face, but today her eyes
were bleary and she looked sad.

"A-a-a-a-CHOO!" Grandma
sneezed when she saw Mia.

"Bless you!" said Mia. She hopped onto the cushion she'd just made and leaned her front paws on the edge of the bed. "Dad said you weren't feeling well, so I've come to keep you company."

"Ah, thank you, Mia," replied Grandma, wiping her nose on a white daisy petal. Then she sneezed again. "A-a-a-CHOO!"

"Oh, dear. You must be feeling awful," Mia said.

12

"Yes, I am." Grandma sighed.

"My poor nose is so sore . . .

a-a-a-CHOO!"

Mia tilted her head to one side.

"Would you like me to tell you a story?"

Grandma's eyes lit up. "Ooh, yes, please! I do love your stor— a-a-a-CHOO!"

Mia sat back on her cushion. If she could think of a really good story, Grandma might forget about her sneezes and her sore nose.

Mia's whiskers wiggled with excitement as a story began to form in her mind: "Once upon a

14

time . . . there was a caterpillar!"
she started.

"A caterpillar? Well, I never,"
said Grandma with a loud sniff.

"And she was named
Clarissa!" said Mia.

"That's a big name for a little
caterpillar," said Grandma.

"Oh, but she wasn't little!"
cried Mia, and her whiskers
twitched and wiggled so much
she had to jump down and run

around Grandma's bed. "She was the biggest caterpillar you've ever seen! She was bigger than you and me and Mom and Dad and all the babies put together!"

"Goodness," said Grandma. Then she smiled. She hadn't sneezed for quite a while now. "How did she get to be so big?"

"Well . . . ," began Mia, jumping back onto the cushion, "Clarissa was very

greedy. She ate and ate and ate, all day long."

17

Grandma frowned. "Wherever did she get all that food from?"

Mia's whiskers quivered as she thought up the answer. "Clarissa had a best friend. His name was Archie, and he was a tiny ant. Archie brought Clarissa lots of snacks. He brought her leaves and berries and nuts and—"

"Lucky Clarissa!" said Grandma, wriggling upright. She looked much happier now.

Mia sat up on her hind legs as the next part of the story came into her head. "But one day—and this is the really scary bit of the story, Grandma—Clarissa disappeared!"

"Oh, dear!" said Grandma. "Where had she gone?"

Mia sighed. "Nobody knew. Archie searched all through Misty Wood, but he couldn't find her anywhere."

19

Grandma shook her head, and her whiskers began to droop. "That's a very sad story."

Mia was about to explain that she hadn't finished yet when her mom came scampering over to them.

"Thank you for looking after Grandma, Mia," she said. "The babies are asleep now, so I'll take over from you."

Mia sighed. She was just

20

getting to the most exciting part of
the story.

"It's all right, Mom, *I'm*
looking after Grandma," she said.

Mia's mom smiled. Then she
stroked the moss cushion that Mia
had just made. "What a lovely soft
cushion. Well done, Mia. There's
just one thing—"

"Oh, Mom, I'm in the middle
of telling Grandma a story!" Mia
interrupted.

"I know," Mia's mom said.
"But I just need you to fetch
something for me."

Mia sighed. She wanted to go
on with her story. She wanted
to give it the best, most exciting
ending ever so that Grandma
would forget all about being sick.

"It's all right, Mia," Grandma
said. "I'm feeling a bit tired, so I'll
have a nap and you can tell me the
rest later. I'll look forward to that."

Grandma yawned and curled up in her lovely warm bed, ready to fall fast asleep.

Mia thought about where Clarissa the caterpillar could have disappeared to, so she could tell her grandma later.

"I need you to bring me some bluebells," Mia's mom said. "You can do that, can't you, Mia?"

"Easy-peasy," said Mia.

But she was still thinking about

the story. *Where, oh, where would Archie find Clarissa?*

Mia's mom looked at her. "Are you sure you won't forget? I know what you're like when you're making up one of your stories— you never have room in your head to think about anything else! Try to remember: I need you to get me some bluebells."

"Yes, yes, bluebells, I know, Mom," Mia said as she hopped

24

down from the cushion. *Maybe Clarissa could be hiding in a big, spooky cave? Maybe she got caught in a giant cobweb?*

"Sleep well, Grandma," Mia called as she scampered through the burrow. *Maybe Clarissa got stuck inside a rabbit hole?*

Mia raced through the tunnel that led into Misty Wood. She jumped out of the little hole between the roots, opened her

gauzy wings, and floated up, up,
up into the sunshine.

"Clarissa the Giant Caterpillar!
My best story ever!" the little Moss
Mouse squeaked happily as she
fluttered away.

CHAPTER TWO

Don't Forget . . .

Mia's wings glimmered and shone as she flew through the bright sunlight.

"I can't forget," she muttered

to herself. "Mom wants me to bring her some . . . ooh! What's that?"

Bright green leaves were hanging down from an oak tree nearby. They had huge holes in them, as if something had been eating them.

"Maybe a giant caterpillar ate those leaves!" Mia gasped. Her whiskers were twitching like mad. "Maybe it was Clarissa!"

She swooped down to take a closer look.

The leaves did look just like Clarissa had been chomping them with her greedy munching jaws.

Mia landed on the tree branch and skipped along it. Maybe she would find a real-life Clarissa up

here! She searched everywhere, peering under the leaves, but she couldn't see a giant caterpillar.

I'm just like Archie the Ant! Mia thought with a smile. *I'm hunting for Clarissa!*

Mia leaped off the branch and flitted between the trees. She had to get home to the burrow right away to tell Grandma the next part of her story. But . . . wait a minute!

The little Moss Mouse came

to a halt. Her mom had asked her to get something. What was it? She thought and thought, but she couldn't remember. Her head was too full of thoughts about Clarissa and Archie.

"Think, Mia, think!" she squeaked.

I need you to bring me some b . . .

It was no good. Next, she tried saying it out loud: "I need you to bring me some b . . ." But, try as

she might, she couldn't remember what it was.

"It's something beginning with *B*," Mia said, scratching her furry head.

The little Moss Mouse looked at the trees and plants that were growing all around her. Then she started to smile. "There must be lots of things in Misty Wood that begin with *B*," she said to herself. "If I keep looking for them, I'm

bound to remember what it was
that Mom wanted."

She swirled her wings and
whizzed off. Before long, she saw
a fluffy brown fairy animal with
floppy ears and beautiful golden
wings hopping along the ground.

"A Bud Bunny!" Mia cried.
"That begins with a *B*!"

She watched the bunny leaping
over ferns. Why would her mom
want a Bud Bunny? It looked much

too bouncy for the inside of Mia's burrow. And there weren't any buds there for it to open into flowers, which was the Bud Bunnies' special job.

"It can't be a Bud Bunny," Mia said, shaking her head.

Then she saw a big beech tree with wide branches stretching out like huge arms.

"Oooh—I know!" Mia cried, clapping her little paws together. "A beechwood back scratcher! Mom always has an itchy back."

But then Mia remembered that her dad had made her mom a beautiful back scratcher from a piece of beechwood only the other day.

35

"I don't think Mom would want *another* back scratcher," Mia said. "After all, she's only got one back!"

She flew on through the woods until she saw some water glinting in the sunlight.

"A babbling brook!" Mia squeaked. "Mom would love one of those!"

She glided down and landed softly on the bank of the brook. The water was fresh and clear and

made a cheerful gurgling noise as it

rushed along.

Mia scampered across the

bank. She sat down and leaned over

to catch some of the water in her

paws.

"Zzzz!"

Mia jumped and nearly

tumbled into the brook. Something

was buzzing around her head!

"Beeeeee careful," a buzzy

voice said to her. "You don't want

37

to fall in." Then it stopped buzzing and landed on the bank in front of Mia. It was a fat, stripy bumblebee!

"Whatever are you doing?" the bee asked.

"I'm trying to catch the water," Mia told him. "My mom wants me to bring her a babbling brook."

"Well, that'zzz very strange," said the bumblebee. "Thizzz brook flowzzz on for milezzz and milezzz. It'zzz much too big to carry home."

Mia sighed. "Maybe I've got it wrong. All I know for sure is that she wants me to get her something beginning with *B*."

The bumblebee frowned.

"Your mom muzzzt have meant zzzomething elzzze," he buzzed.

Mia looked at him, and her whiskers started to tremble with excitement. "I know! Maybe Mom asked me to bring her a bumblebee!"

"Oh, I don't think so," the bee buzzed, backing away from Mia.

"We've got a lovely burrow," Mia said. "You'd really like it."

"But I need to be outzide, making lotzz of lovely honey from

flower nectar," he replied with a frown.

"Oh yes." Mia's whiskers began to droop. "Sorry, I didn't mean to upset you. It's probably not a bumblebee Mom wants after all. I just wish I could remember what it was."

She sat down on the grass and sniffed. She was feeling very fed up indeed. Her mom would be angry if she didn't remember!

The bumblebee rubbed his face with his front legs. "Don't be sad," he said. "What'z your name?"

Mia looked up at him. "Mia," she said quietly.

"I'm Buzby," he said. "Buzby the bumblebee. Look, Mia, there are loadzz of thingzz in Misty Wood beginning with *B*. I could help you look for them."

"Oh, thank you, Buzby!" Mia fluttered into the air.

"And just in case it *iz* a bumblebee she'z after," Buzby went on, "I'll come back with you to your burrow when we've finished looking. But only for a vizit. How about that?"

"That's so kind of you, Buzby," Mia said. She flapped her tiny wings happily. "Let's go!"

CHAPTER THREE

Searching Misty Wood!

Mia and Buzby fluttered through the Heart of Misty Wood looking for things beginning with *B*. All around them, sunbeams poked

through the leaves like long golden fingers, making pretty patterns on the ground.

"Hey, Buzby!" Mia called. "There's a birch tree. That begins with a *B*."

The bumblebee zoomed over to the tall birch tree that Mia was pointing to. Beautiful pictures of hearts and rainbows had been carved into its silver bark by the Bark Badgers.

"Too big," Buzby buzzed. "It'll never fit inside your burrow."

But Mia's whiskers were twitching. "What about the twigs? We could make a bristly broomstick

46

with them! Maybe that's what Mom wants."

Buzby looked doubtful. "Doezn't she have one already?" he asked.

Mia nodded. "Yes, she does. She sweeps the burrow with it every day."

"Then she won't need another one, will she? We'll have to look for something elze."

They fluttered their wings and flew on until they came to a

sunny clearing. A herd of Dream Deer were bounding across the grass. Their legs were so long and they moved so gracefully that they looked as if they were dancing. Mia's whiskers twitched and twizzled. Her next idea was so much fun!

"Maybe Mom wants a ballet-dancing buffalo!" she squeaked. She was so excited she turned head over heels in the air.

SEARCHING MISTY WOOD!

Buzby looked very surprised. "A buffalo? In Misty Wood? I've never seen one. Have you?"

"No, I suppose not," Mia said, spinning the right way up again.

"Your imagination'z running away with you," said Buzby. "Let'z head back. Keep looking for thingz beginning with *B*!"

Mia followed him through the trees. Buzby was a very serious bumblebee. Maybe she could think

of a story that would make him laugh. Her whiskers twizzled like mad.

"How about a boggley boogaloo!" she squeaked.

Buzby stared at Mia. "You just made that up, didn't you?" he buzzed.

"Yes, I did!" Mia giggled. Her whiskers twitched as more ideas popped into her head. "A boogaloo's a bright yellow bug, with big boggley eyes. And he

loves to . . . he loves to boogie! I could tell you a story about him if you like. . . ."

But Buzby wasn't listening. He'd seen something up ahead and he was zooming toward it, dodging between the tree trunks.

"Mia!" he called. "Come and zee!"

Mia's wings sparkled as she hurried after him.

"What did you find?"

"Down there," buzzed Buzby.

Mia looked down and saw a bramble bush stretching its thorny arms around the trunk of a tree. In between the thorns she could see . . .

"Blackberries!" she cried.

The two of them landed next to the bush. Sure enough, there were lots of juicy blackberries growing there, as shiny and bright as jewels.

"Are these what your mom wanted?" asked Buzby.

Mia scratched her head with her tiny pink paw. "I'm not sure," she said. "They do look delicious, though. Why don't we take some back to the burrow, just in case.

54

But there are so many—how will we carry them?"

Buzby twirled his antennae. "We need a bazket."

Mia's whiskers twitched. "Oh, Buzby—*basket* begins with *B*, too! Do you think that's what Mom wants?"

"I don't know," said Buzby. "But I know just where we can find one. Come on!"

He spun his little wings and

55

leaped into the air, flying swiftly
toward the edge of Misty Wood.
Mia followed him, and soon the
trees began to thin out and she saw
a long, leafy hedgerow.

There wasn't a basket to be
seen. In fact, there wasn't anything
at all beginning with *B*!

"Why did we come out here,
Buzby?" she called out.

"Follow me," he buzzed, "and
you'll see!"

CHAPTER FOUR

Follow the Song!

"Come on," Buzby called, pointing with his front legs as he flew up to the top of the hedge.

Mia raced after him. "Wow!" she gasped.

Hundreds of tiny, glittering dewdrops dangled from spiderwebs on the other side of the hedge. They looked like strings of diamonds.

"Those dewdrops are beautiful!" Mia cried. "What a shame they don't begin with *B*. Mom would love them!"

A white kitten with pale blue wings flew up to Mia. She was carrying a little basket made from woven flower stems.

58

Mia's whiskers began to twirl. "You're a Cobweb Kitten, aren't you?" she said.

The kitten nodded.

"It's your job to decorate the spiderwebs," Mia went on.

"That's right," purred the kitten.

59

"You've done such a lovely job!" Mia said.

"Thank you." The kitten smiled. "Do help yourself to some of my dewdrops."

"It's a bazket we need," Buzby interrupted. "We're looking for thingz beginning with *B*."

Mia nodded. "My mom asked me to bring her something beginning with *B*, and I've forgotten what it is," she explained

to the kitten. "We've found some lovely blackberries, but there are too many for us to carry. If we had a basket to put the blackberries in, we'd have two things beginning with *B*!"

"You can have my basket if you like," the friendly kitten said. "It's very light, and I've got loads more at home. I'll just hang these last few dewdrops."

Mia watched as the kitten flew

up and strung the bright droplets
on the spider silk.

"Blackberries—how delicious,"
the kitten purred as she handed the
empty basket to Mia. "I bet your
mom will love them."

"I think so, too," Mia said. "I
just hope they're what she asked me
for. Thank you for your help!"

"Good luck," called the kitten
as Mia and Buzby headed back to
the blackberry bush.

"I hope we *will* be lucky," said Mia when they got back to the bush and began filling the basket.

"Shhh!" whispered Buzby. "Lizzen!"

High above their heads, a bird was singing.

"Twee-twee! Twee-twee-twee!"

Mia looked up. A little bird with bright blue feathers the color of a summer sky was circling high above them.

63

"A bluebird!"
Mia cried. "Maybe
that's what Mom
wanted. Quick, we've
got to catch up with him!"

Gripping the basket tightly in

her paws, Mia flew as fast as she could. But the little bird was too quick. His blue feathers flashed through the treetops as he darted away, singing, "Twee-twee! Twee-twee-twee!"

"Follow the song!" cried Mia.

"Phew!" panted Buzby, spinning his wings so fast they disappeared in a blur. "We'll never catch up with him!"

Suddenly, Buzby slowed down

and sniffed the air. "Ooh, Mia—
what'z that lovely smell?"

A beautiful blue carpet of
flowers stretched out on the ground
below them. Mia and Buzby were
flying over Bluebell Glade. But
Mia didn't have time to think about

lovely smells. She just wanted to
catch up with the bluebird.

"Come on, Buzby! Don't slow
down!" she called.

"I've never seen so many
flowerz before," panted Buzby.

"Twee-twee!" sang the bluebird,

far ahead of them. His voice was getting fainter.

"Quick!" cried Mia. "We're going to lose him!"

"I wish we could go and pick some," Buzby sighed, looking down at Bluebell Glade. "They smell so nice."

"Buzby, forget the flowers!" Mia cried. "Come on!"

But, try as they might, Mia and Buzby couldn't keep up with

the bluebird. They whizzed along until they came to Heather Hill. The bluebird had disappeared. They couldn't even hear his song anymore.

"Do you think we could stop for a minute?" puffed Buzby. "I'm not used to flying so fast."

They flopped down on a patch of grass in among the heather. Lots of little yellow flowers were growing there, but Mia didn't notice them.

She felt really sad. She was quite sure that her mom had asked her for a bluebird, and now they had lost him.

Mia tried to cheer herself up by thinking about her story for Grandma. Maybe in the next part of the story, Archie the Ant could come to Heather Hill to search for his friend Clarissa. Maybe he'd look for her through the dark, shadowy places beneath the heather.

Mia peered between the twisty roots, imagining the little ant scurrying back and forth. There was no sign of Clarissa, but Mia noticed something else. Something blue.

"Buzby, what's that?" she said, pointing her paw at it.

"I'm not sure," Buzby replied. "I'll see if I can get it."

Buzby flattened his wings and squeezed between the heather plants. He came back holding a

beautiful bright blue feather in his antennae.

"It must have fallen when the bluebird flew over the hill," he said.

"It's so soft." Mia stroked the feather with her paw. "Maybe Mom wanted a bluebird's *feather*," she said, placing it in the basket. "But we'd better keep on looking for other things that begin with *B*."

"I begin with *B*!" a voice called out.

Mia was so surprised, she dropped the basket on her paw. "Who said that?" she squeaked as she rubbed her toe.

73

But there was no one there, just
the little yellow flowers growing in
the grass. Mia stared at them. They
were buttercups. And *buttercups*
began with *B*! It must have been a
buttercup that spoke to her.

Mia picked some of the flowers
and put them in the basket on
top of the blackberries and the
bluebird's feather.

"No!" came the voice again.
"Not them, *me*!"

The voice was calling from up above. Whoever it was sounded very mad.

"Who's that?" Mia squeaked in her bravest voice, and she half covered her head with the basket.

CHAPTER FIVE

Seeing Stars

"Please don't hide," said the voice.

Mia peeped out from under

the little basket. An insect with big

purple wings was floating in the

air, gazing down at her with huge
eyes.

It was a beautiful butterfly.

"Hello!" the butterfly said,
swishing her wings. "I only shouted

at you because I was so excited. You see, I didn't always begin with *B*. In fact, up until last week, I began with *C*."

Mia and Buzby stared at the butterfly, puzzled.

"What do you mean?" Mia asked.

"Well, I used to be a caterpillar. But *now* I'm a beautiful, brilliant, brightly colored butterfly—so I most definitely begin with *B*!"

Mia's heart gave a big jump inside her. "Your name isn't Clarissa, is it?" she asked.

The butterfly looked surprised. "No. It's Buffy. Why do you ask?"

"Oh, never mind. It's just something to do with a story," Mia said. "It's very nice to meet you, Buffy. My name's Mia, and this is my friend Buzby."

"Nice to meet you, too," said Buffy.

Mia put her basket down and began to explain how her mom had asked her for something beginning with *B*. "I just can't remember what it was, though," she finished with a sigh.

"It might be blackberriez," Buzby said. "Or buttercupz. Or possibly a bumblebee like me. Or perhapz a bazket, or a bluebird'z feather, or—"

"A butterfly!" Mia interrupted,

her whiskers wiggling with excitement.

"Really?" Buffy looked pleased. "Well, of course, I *am* one of the most beautiful butterflies in Misty Wood, so I wouldn't be at all surprised if it *is* me your mom wants. Why don't I come along with you?"

"Oh yes, would you?" Mia cried. "I know my mom would love your gorgeous wings."

"You could help us look for other thingz beginning with *B*, too," Buzby said, and he got up from the grass and stretched out his little legs. "Come on, let'z head back into Misty Wood!"

Buzby and Mia flew up to join Buffy as she fluttered off toward the trees. But Mia was so busy admiring Buffy's dazzling purple wings that she didn't look where she was going. All of a sudden—

oomph!—she flew straight into a big tree trunk. "Ouch!" squeaked Mia as she slid down the trunk and landed with a thud.

"Oh no! Did you hurt yourself?" asked Buzby, landing softly on the ground beside her.

"Oooh," said Mia, "what lovely twinkly stars . . . pink ones and silver ones and—"

"Starz?" said Buzby, looking around. "Where?"

"She's seeing stars because she bumped her head," Buffy explained, fanning Mia with her wings. "Are you okay?"

"Yes, I think so," Mia said,

sitting up carefully. The stars had all disappeared now. "It wasn't a bad bump. Thanks, Buffy."

Something had fallen off the tree as Mia slid down it. She picked it up. It was a piece of bark.

"Maybe it was some bark Mom wanted!" she said.

She turned the bark over and saw that it was covered in swirly lines and circles.

"What a beautiful pattern.

A Bark Badger must have made it," Buffy said.

"Hey!" a gruff voice called.

Mia jumped in surprise. A stocky Bark Badger with a black-and-white-striped face and shiny silver wings was coming toward them. It must have been his tree she'd bumped into! "I'm so s-s-sorry!" she stammered. "I didn't mean to knock your bark off the tree. It was an accident, I promise."

86

The badger threw back his head and gave a loud, hearty laugh.

"Don't worry, little Moss Mouse," he said in a booming voice. "You can keep that piece if you like."

Mia heaved a sigh of relief. "Thanks!" she said. "My friends and I are collecting as many things beginning with *B* as we can find—for my mom."

"I see." The Bark Badger nodded kindly. "Can I help?" he asked.

"Wait a minute!" Buffy's purple wings started to quiver. "It might be a *Bark Badger* that your mom wants, Mia."

Mia looked at the badger's big shoulders and his rough gray fur. It would be a tight squeeze fitting him into the burrow—but maybe Buffy was right.

"It *could* be a Bark Badger," she said. "But I'm not sure. Oh, I wish I could remember!"

89

The badger smiled. "Well, why don't I come with you?" he said. "Just in case it *is* a Bark Badger you need. My name's Barney, by the way."

"Thank you so much!" Mia cried. "Look at everything we've collected!"

She held up her little pink paws and began counting on her fingers.

"A bumblebee, a butterfly, a Bark Badger, a bluebird's feather,

90

a piece of bark, and a basket full
of buttercups and blackberries!"
She looked at her new friends
and smiled. "I think we must have
everything beginning with *B* in the
whole of Misty Wood. Thank you,
everyone!"

The others smiled.

Buzby looked up at the sky.
"The sun'z going down," he said.
"Iz it teatime yet?"

"It must be," said Mia. "Come

on, let's head back to the burrow.
I bet Mom's made a cake."

Barney picked up the basket,
and the four friends flew off
through Misty Wood, with Mia
leading the way.

CHAPTER SIX

Two Happy Endings

Mia scampered down the tunnel that led to her burrow, her new friends close behind her. "Come meet my mom, everyone!" she called.

Mia's mom looked up in surprise as first Mia, then Buzby, then Buffy, and finally Barney squeezed into the burrow.

"Well, I'm very glad I made such a big cake for tea," she said. "Mia, did you remember to bring—"

But Mia didn't let her mom finish. "I've brought lots of things!" she squeaked excitedly. "Let's go over to Grandma's bed, and I'll show them to you!"

Mia's mom looked puzzled.

Mia scampered over, with Buzby flying along at her side.

"I do hope we got the thing my mom wanted," she whispered to him.

"I'm sure you did," Buzby hummed, close to her ear. "We have so many thingz beginning with *B*."

Grandma's little black eyes nearly popped out of her head when she saw all the visitors.

"Well, well, well!" she said. "This is a surprise! Pull up a cushion, why don't you? There's plenty of them."

Barney the Bark Badger grinned as he sat down. He was much too big to stand up in the burrow. He kept bumping his wings on the ceiling.

Mia looked at her mom. "I know you wanted something beginning with *B*," she started

to explain, "but I forgot what it was. So I brought you everything beginning with *B* that I could find. There's a bumblebee. . . ."

Buzby stood up and gave a little bow. "Buzby, at your service, ma'am," he said.

"Lovely to meet you, Buzby," Mia's mom said. "But I'm afraid it wasn't a bumblebee I wanted."

"Well, how about a butterfly?" asked Mia. "This is Buffy."

Buffy gave a twirl so that everyone could see her pretty lilac wings.

Mia's mom shook her head. "You look lovely, Buffy. But it wasn't a butterfly I was after."

"Oh, dear." Mia was beginning to feel worried. "Was it a Bark Badger, Mom? Because I brought Barney just in case."

Barney raised a front paw. "How do you do?" he said

grandly. "I'm very happy to help out however I can."

"That's very good of you," Mia's mom said. "But I'm afraid I don't need a Bark Badger, either."

Mia bit her lip. This wasn't going well at all. She picked up the basket.

"How about this lovely basket?"

Mia's mom shook her head.

Mia's whiskers drooped down below her mouth.

100

"Show her what'z inside the bazket!" Buzby buzzed quietly. "There are still lotz of thingz beginning with *B*."

"Okay," Mia whispered. She pulled out the bluebird's feather and showed it to her mom. "Was it this?"

"No, Mia," her mom replied. "But that's a nice feather. I can weave it into the quilt I'm making for the babies' cot."

101

"What about this?" Mia held up the piece of bark.

"Bark's always useful," Mia's mom said. "And I love the pattern. But I didn't ask for a piece of bark. What I wanted was—"

"These?" Mia squeaked, tipping up the basket so that all the juicy blackberries spilled out.

"No, not blackberries, though they'll be lovely to have with our tea," Mia's mom said.

There was just one thing left.

"Buttercups!" cried Mia, holding up the bunch of bright yellow flowers. "Please tell me you wanted buttercups!"

Mia's mom sighed. "No, Mia. I'm sorry, but it wasn't buttercups I asked you to bring, either."

Mia sat back on her hind legs and sighed. "What in Misty Wood could it be? I thought I'd collected *everything* beginning with *B*."

"Bluebells," Mia's mom said gently. "I asked for some bluebells."

"Some *bluebells*?" Mia gasped.

"Oh no!" groaned Buzby. He hid his face in his front legs. "Mia—

we flew over hundredz of them in Bluebell Glade . . ."

Mia nodded. "Yes, when we were chasing the bluebird. We didn't stop to think. What do you want the bluebells for, Mom?"

"To put on the cushion you made for Grandma," Mia's mom said. "All it needs are some bluebell decorations to make it quite perfect."

"Grandma, I'm so sorry!" Mia burst into tears. "I've been a silly

105

Moss Mouse. Your cushion would have looked so pretty with some bluebells to finish it off!"

Grandma's nose wrinkled in a smile.

"Don't cry, Mia," she said. "I'm not upset that you forgot about the bluebells. Because you *did* bring some buttercups—and they're my favorite flowers in the world!"

"Really?" Mia sniffed.

"Really and truly," her

106

grandma replied. "They're so very bright and cheerful, they make me think of sunshine. I'd much rather have buttercups than bluebells on my cushion."

Mia wiped her eyes and fixed some of the buttercups onto Grandma's moss cushion. They looked beautiful, and everybody clapped and cheered.

"Well done," said Mia's mom. "You might have forgotten the

bluebells, Mia, but you've made Grandma very happy with those buttercups. Now, shall I get the tea?"

Buzby, Buffy, and Barney all said they would help.

"I'll come, too!" Mia said.

Grandma shook her head. "Stay here with me, Mia," she said. "I want to hear the rest of your story. Sit on the buttercup cushion beside me and tell me more about Clarissa the Caterpillar."

Mia jumped onto the cushion. "D'you remember, Grandma, how Clarissa disappeared, and her friend Archie the Ant couldn't find her?" she asked.

Grandma nodded.

"Well . . ." Mia's whiskers wiggled. She told Grandma how Archie had searched everywhere. He'd climbed up a big tall tree— how scary that was! And he'd hunted all through the roots of the

heather plants on Heather Hill, but Clarissa was nowhere to be seen.

"So where was she?" Grandma asked.

Mia's whiskers were twizzling so much. She knew Grandma would love the end of the story.

"There was one place Archie hadn't looked—Moonshine Pond. He trudged all the way there through Misty Wood. His legs were aching so much he could hardly walk."

"Poor Archie," said Grandma. "I feel quite sorry for him."

"When he got to the pond, there was no sign of Clarissa," Mia went on. "There was only a beautiful butterfly admiring her reflection in the water. Archie started to cry. 'I miss my friend Clarissa!' he said. The butterfly flew over and sat beside him on the grass. 'Don't be sad,' she said. 'It's me. *I'm* Clarissa.'"

"Well, I never!" Grandma said.

"Archie didn't believe her," continued Mia. "But Clarissa explained that all caterpillars eat lots and lots and get bigger and bigger, and then they disappear for a while until they turn into butterflies. She thanked Archie for bringing her all those lovely snacks to eat when she had been a caterpillar.

"'You've helped me become the

112

most beautiful butterfly in Misty Wood,' she said. 'I'll be your best friend for ever and ever.' Archie was so happy he forgot how tired he was and danced all the way around Moonshine Pond. The end!"

"Oh, Mia!" said Grandma with a big smile. "I love a happy ending."

"Did I hear someone say 'snacks'?" called Mia's mom. She trotted up to Grandma's bed,

carrying the piece of bark. On top of it was a cake made from crunchy hazelnuts.

Buzby and Buffy followed her, carrying acorns filled with blackberry juice. Mia's dad came over, too, with some plump barleycorns he'd found while he was out collecting moss.

And last of all came Barney, who was carrying Mia's baby brothers and sisters in the basket

so that they could join in the tea party.

Everybody sat down around Grandma and began eating and drinking. Mia snuggled up with Grandma in her mossy bed, and nibbled some cake.

"Look at all the things I found!" she said when she had finished her cake. "A bumblebee, blackberries, a basket, and a butterfly . . ."

"I can think of something else beginning with *B*," Grandma whispered when Mia got to the end of the list.

"What?" asked Mia, looking around. She saw the grains of barley that her dad had brought.

"Is it *barleycorns*, Grandma?"

"They're tasty, but no, that's not what I meant," Grandma said.

Then Mia saw her four brothers and sisters sipping their blackberry

117

juice. "Do you mean *babies*, Grandma?"

Grandma laughed. "That's a good guess! But no. You've brought so many wonderful things today, Mia—especially those beautiful buttercups. But the most special thing of all is that I feel *better*. You told me such a lovely story and made me such a beautiful cushion that I forgot all about my cold. It's quite gone away! You've made me

118

feel *better*, and that's the *best* thing
of all."

Mia looked at Grandma's
smiling face. Then she looked at
her mom, who was showing
Buzby and Buffy and Barney
how to make a moss cushion.
They weren't very good at it,
and everybody was laughing and
giggling as they rolled the moss
around. Then she looked at her
dad, who was tickling the babies

with the bluebird's feather and

making them laugh.

Everybody was so happy.

Perhaps I'm not so silly after all, Mia thought, and she cuddled up next to Grandma and helped herself to another piece of her mom's delicious cake.

Turn the page for
lots of fun
Misty Wood
activities!

Mia's mom asked her
to find some bluebells.
Can you help Mia follow
the right path?

Mia spent the day in Misty Wood trying to find things beginning with *B*. She found lots and lots of things!

Why not go on a treasure hunt in your garden, or in the park with your parent or guardian?

Write down all the things you find.

Things beginning with A

_____

_____

_____

Things beginning with B

_____

_____

_____

Things beginning with C

_____

_____

_____

Spot the Difference

The picture on the opposite page is slightly different from this one. Can you circle all the differences?

Moss Mice, like Mia, love making and decorating soft, beautiful moss cushions for the fairy animals to sleep on.

Use the outline on the next page to design and decorate your very own moss cushion!

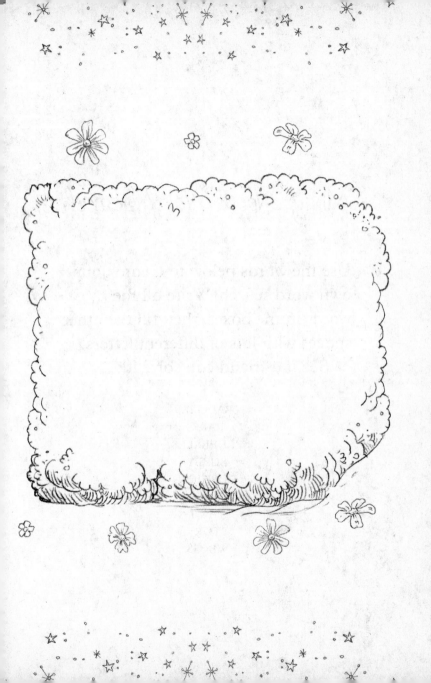

Misty Wood Word Search

Use the words below to create your own word search! Write all the words in the boxes, then fill the other spaces with lots of different letters. See if a friend can solve it!

BADGER
BARK
BLUEBELLS
BUZBY
CUSHION
MOSS
PAWS
STORY
WINGS

Fairy Animals

of Misty Wood

Poppy the Pony

Lily Small

Henry Holt and Company
New York

With special thanks to Thea Bennett

Henry Holt and Company
Publishers since 1866
175 Fifth Avenue
New York, New York 10010
mackids.com

First published in the United States in 2016 by Henry Holt and Company.
Originally published in Great Britain in 2014 by Egmont UK Limited.

Library of Congress Cataloging-in-Publication Data is available.
Paper Over Board ISBN 978-1-250-11398-6
Paperback ISBN 978-1-250-11399-3

Our books may be purchased in bulk for promotional, educational, or business use.
Please contact your local bookseller or the Macmillan Corporate
and Premium Sales Department at (800) 221-7945 ext. 5442
or by e-mail at MacmillanSpecialMarkets@macmillan.com.

First American Edition—2016
Printed in the United States of America by
LSC Communications, Harrisonburg, Virginia

Hardcover
1 3 5 7 9 10 8 6 4 2

Paperback
5 7 9 10 8 6 4

Contents

CHAPTER ONE

Poppy Needs a Friend

It was a lovely bright morning in Misty Wood. On top of Sundown Hill, a little pony called Poppy was grazing beside her mom.

Sundown Hill was the sunniest place in the whole wood. The yellow primroses that grew there shone like sunbeams, and there was plenty of lush green grass, too. Poppy liked the grass very much.

"Yum, yum!" she whinnied as she nibbled the juicy stems. She was nearly full now, but the grass was so tasty she couldn't stop eating.

"That's right, Poppy!" neighed her mom. "We've got lots of work

3

to do today, so you need a big
breakfast."

Poppy was a Petal Pony—
one of the fairy animals of Misty
Wood. Her gleaming coat was the
same pale yellow as the primroses
and her silky mane and tail were
as white as swan feathers. It was
the Petal Ponies' special job to
swish their glossy tails and waft
the beautiful scent of the flowers
through the wood. The sweet smells

made all the other animals feel happy.

"*Woof, woof!*" Loud barking rang out across the hill.

Poppy stopped chewing and turned to see who it was.

"Let's have a race!" a voice called. "I bet I win. *Woof!*"

Poppy heard the patter of paws on the ground. Lots of paws! Her long legs started to tremble as a pack of Pollen Puppies came

5

scampering through the tall grass.

"*Woof!*" they barked as they charged along with their tails wagging. "Hello, Petal Pony. *Woof, woof!*"

But instead of answering, all Poppy could think was *Help!*

You see, Poppy was a very shy pony, and she found it hard to talk to fairy animals she didn't know. Quick as a flash, she unfurled her sky-blue wings

and flew behind her mom to hide.

"Hey, Petal Pony!" barked one of the puppies. "Where did you go?" He peeped through the silky fronds of Poppy's mom's long tail. When he saw Poppy hiding, he trotted around to speak to her.

"There you are," he said with a grin. "We're having a race to Honeydew Meadow. Would you like to come with us?"

Poppy shook her head.

"Why don't you, Poppy?" said her mom. "You're really good at galloping."

"Yes, you could win the race," barked the puppy. "Come on!"

Poppy hid her face in her long white mane. She felt so shy, she didn't know what to do.

Poppy's mom looked at her kindly. "It'll be fun," she said.

Poppy thought for a moment. Her legs were a lot longer than a

puppy's. And she did love to gallop fast. . . .

"Poppy?" Her mom gave her a nudge with her velvety nose. "What do you say?"

Poppy took a deep breath. She wanted to say, "Yes, please. I'd love to!" But her throat went tight and all that came out was a little snuffling noise that sounded like: "*Hm-hm-hm.*"

The puppy wagged his tail.

10

"What did you say? Are you coming?"

Poppy hung her head. She was so embarrassed she felt hot all over.

Poppy's mom looked at her, waiting for her to say something, but Poppy's voice had completely disappeared.

"Maybe not today," Poppy's mom told the puppy. "But thank you very much for asking."

"That's okay! Poppy can play

11

anytime." The puppy waved a paw at Poppy to say good-bye. "Come on, puppies, let's go!"

The puppies scampered away over the hill, barking happily.

"I wish I could have gone

with them," Poppy sighed. "But
I'm so shy I can't even speak
to anybody."

Her mom nuzzled her neck.
"You have to try to be a bit braver,
Poppy. How will the other animals
know that you want to be friends
if you don't talk to them?" She
lifted her head and gazed down
the hill at the rest of Misty Wood.
"Never mind now—it's time to start
work," she said. "The sun's shining

and all the flowers are blooming."

Poppy's face brightened. She loved swishing the lovely flower smells around the wood.

Her mom looked thoughtful for a second. "Why don't we split up and go to different places today?" she said. "I'll go to Bluebell Glade. You could start at Heather Hill. There'll be lots of gorgeous heather blossoms there."

"I'd rather be with you,"

14

Poppy said, her tail drooping. She'd never gone without her mom before.

"You'll be fine," her mom told her gently. "And maybe other fairy animals will come and talk to you. You might make a friend."

"Maybe," said Poppy, but she didn't think so. How could she make a friend if all she managed to say was *hm-hm-hm*?

"Just give it a try!" her mom said. "Have a lovely day and I'll see

15

you at supper." She nuzzled Poppy with her nose and then galloped off a little way before opening her wings and soaring into the sky.

Poppy felt a bit lonely, left behind on Sundown Hill. But the sun was shining and she had lots of work to do, so she shook out her white mane, fluttered her wings, and headed off.

Misty Wood looked beautiful as she flew over it. When she arrived

at Heather Hill, she heard a loud buzzing. Hundreds of bumblebees were hovering over the purple heather flowers.

Poppy landed in a quiet spot at the side of the hill and began flicking her snowy-white tail over the flowers. A wonderful sweet smell like honey filled the air.

"*Mmmmm!*" droned the bumblebees. They flew up and began swirling in a huge cloud.

Then they zoomed down to collect pollen, buzzing even more loudly.

Poppy smiled as she listened. The bees sounded really happy, and it was all because of her!

It was time to move on and find some more flowers.

Poppy cantered down Heather Hill and into the trees. They formed a beautiful green archway for her to run through. Thin fingers of sunlight beamed through the leaves

above her, making a pretty golden pattern on the floor.

Poppy felt very content as she raced along. But then, just as she reached a clearing, she saw three large fairy animals with stripy faces and silver wings.

Bark Badgers! Poppy skidded to a halt. They mustn't see her, or they might want to come over and talk. Luckily, she spotted a big honeysuckle bush that she could

20

hide behind. She trotted over to it as quietly as she could.

Poppy peeped through the leaves. The badgers were busy doing their special job, decorating the tree bark.

Poppy watched as one badger scraped his claws over the bark, making a flowing line that looked just like a pony's tail. Another was scratching swirly shapes that made Poppy think of a rushing stream.

21

The smallest badger was making a
circle with lots of marks inside. When
he'd finished, it looked as if a face
was smiling out from the tree trunk.

That's so clever! thought Poppy.
She noticed that the honeysuckle

bush she was hiding behind was
covered in white flowers with long
yellow stems. She sniffed. The
flowers smelled so lovely—even
sweeter than the heather blossoms.
Careful not to make a sound, she

slowly swung her tail back and forth and the scent began to drift toward the badgers. The smallest one looked around.

"Mmmm," he murmured, "something smells nice!"

Poppy stopped swishing her tail and kept very still. After a minute, the badger turned back to his tree trunk and began to draw a new pattern with his claws.

"Phew!" Poppy breathed a

sigh of relief. He hadn't seen her.

The badgers smiled as they sniffed the honeysuckle perfume. One by one, they began carving beautiful pictures of flowers on their trees. They looked so happy. Poppy's work was done.

She started creeping away from the clearing . . . but the smallest badger looked around again. And this time he spotted her!

"Hello," he called, twirling his silver whiskers in greeting.

Poppy wanted to hide, but she was so shy she couldn't move an inch.

The badger smiled. "You're a Petal Pony."

Poppy nodded. She tried to say something, but nothing came out. It was as if all the words inside her had run away.

"Thank you for making

everything smell so good," the badger said.

Poppy swallowed. She *had* to say something!

"You're welcome," she whispered very quietly.

The badger waited, but Poppy couldn't say anything else.

"Well—thanks again," he said with a friendly wave of his paw, and he turned back to his friends.

Poppy's head fell. The three

badgers were having so much fun, chatting and laughing as they made their beautiful patterns. If only she could go and join in.

"I'll never, ever be able to make a friend," she whispered to herself. A silvery tear ran down her primrose cheek and dripped off the end of her velvety nose.

CHAPTER TWO

The Bluebirds' Song

Poppy shook the tears from her
eyes and began to trot through the
bright green ferns that grew
in clusters beneath the trees.

She couldn't keep feeling sad—she had to find some more flowers. Suddenly, she spotted something ahead. It looked like a huge mirror, shining brightly on the ground.

"Moonshine Pond!" Poppy neighed. "And it's daytime, so the Moonbeam Moles will all be fast asleep. At least I won't have to worry about bumping into any of them."

The Moonbeam Moles lived in burrows on the banks of the pond.

Their special job was to catch
moonbeams and place them in
the water to make it glow like a
beautiful pearl. Of course, the moles
could only collect moonbeams after
dark, so they woke up at night and
went to bed during the day. Right
now they would all be tucked in,
fast asleep in their burrows.

Poppy cantered up to the
pond. It was very quiet there. The
only thing that moved was Poppy's

reflection. Her yellow coat and long white mane looked pretty in the gleaming water.

Not far from the pond, Poppy could see little heaps of earth that marked the entrances to the moles' burrows. She went over and bent her head to see if she could hear the moles inside.

A funny grunting and whistling noise was coming up from under the ground.

"*Och, och, phweee . . .*"

"*Phwee, och, och . . .*"

The moles were snoring! They certainly wouldn't disturb her while she did her work.

34

Poppy saw some lavender bushes close by. She trotted over and swung her long tail to and fro over the lilac flowers.

"*Aaaah!*" she heard the moles sigh. "*Mmmmm!*" they breathed as the soothing lavender scent reached their sleepy noses, deep underground.

Poppy smiled. Her work at Moonshine Pond was finished. She flicked her wings and soared up

through the trees, heading for the
Heart of Misty Wood.

Soon she came to a place
where the trees grew very tall.
Beneath the trees was a grassy
glade, and Poppy drifted toward it.
As she landed, the grass felt as soft
as a cushion under her hooves.

High above in the treetops,
Poppy heard the flutter of wings.
She looked up. Two bluebirds had
landed on a branch.

"*Tweet-tweet*," sang one, flicking his bright blue tail.

"*Cheep-cheep*," replied the other, nodding her little blue head.

Poppy pricked her ears to listen to their lovely song. But they were

37

so high up it sounded very faint. If only they would come closer.

Then Poppy had an idea. She walked over to a rose bush that was growing at the edge of the glade. She brushed her tail over the velvety pink petals, and a beautiful scent rolled like mist across the glade.

One of the bluebirds looked down, his head tilted to the side.

Poppy swept her tail over the roses again.

"*Twee-ee-eet!*" sang the bluebird as the perfume drifted up to him. He leaped off the branch and flew down to the grass.

"*Chee-ee-eep!*" trilled his mate as she joined him.

The two birds hopped around and fluttered their blue wings as if they were dancing. They hadn't noticed Poppy.

They like the smell of roses, Poppy thought with a smile.

There was a rustle at the edge of the glade and a shiny brown nose peeped through a cluster of ferns. A Stardust Squirrel with wings as bright as starshine emerged. Poppy darted behind some trees so he wouldn't see her. But then a voice spoke up on the other side of the nearest tree trunk.

"Ho hum, tiddly-pum! Just look at all these leaves . . ."

Poppy peeped around the tree

trunk. A Hedgerow Hedgehog was rolling around on the ground, collecting dead leaves on her spines.

"*Tweet-tweet! Cheep-cheeep!*" warbled the bluebirds.

"What a lovely song!" the hedgehog sighed. "I think I'll take a break." She sat down to listen. She still had leaves stuck all over her back like a coat.

Who's going to turn up next? thought Poppy. She made herself as

small as she could so the hedgehog wouldn't notice her.

"*Tweety-tweet-cheep!*" trilled the bluebirds.

Now Poppy could hear rustling noises all around her. She felt her heart beating fast. There were fairy animals everywhere, making their way into the glade. A herd of Dream Deer trotted past, lifting their graceful heads as they sniffed the roses. Some Bark Badgers

pushed their stripy faces through the ferns to watch the birds. Pollen Puppies, tails wagging, flopped on the ground to listen.

More and more animals arrived. Cobweb Kittens floated down through the air. Moss Mice and Holly Hamsters fluttered out from behind the trees, their tiny wings twinkling.

"*Tweeety-tweet! Cheepy-cheep!*" sang the bluebirds.

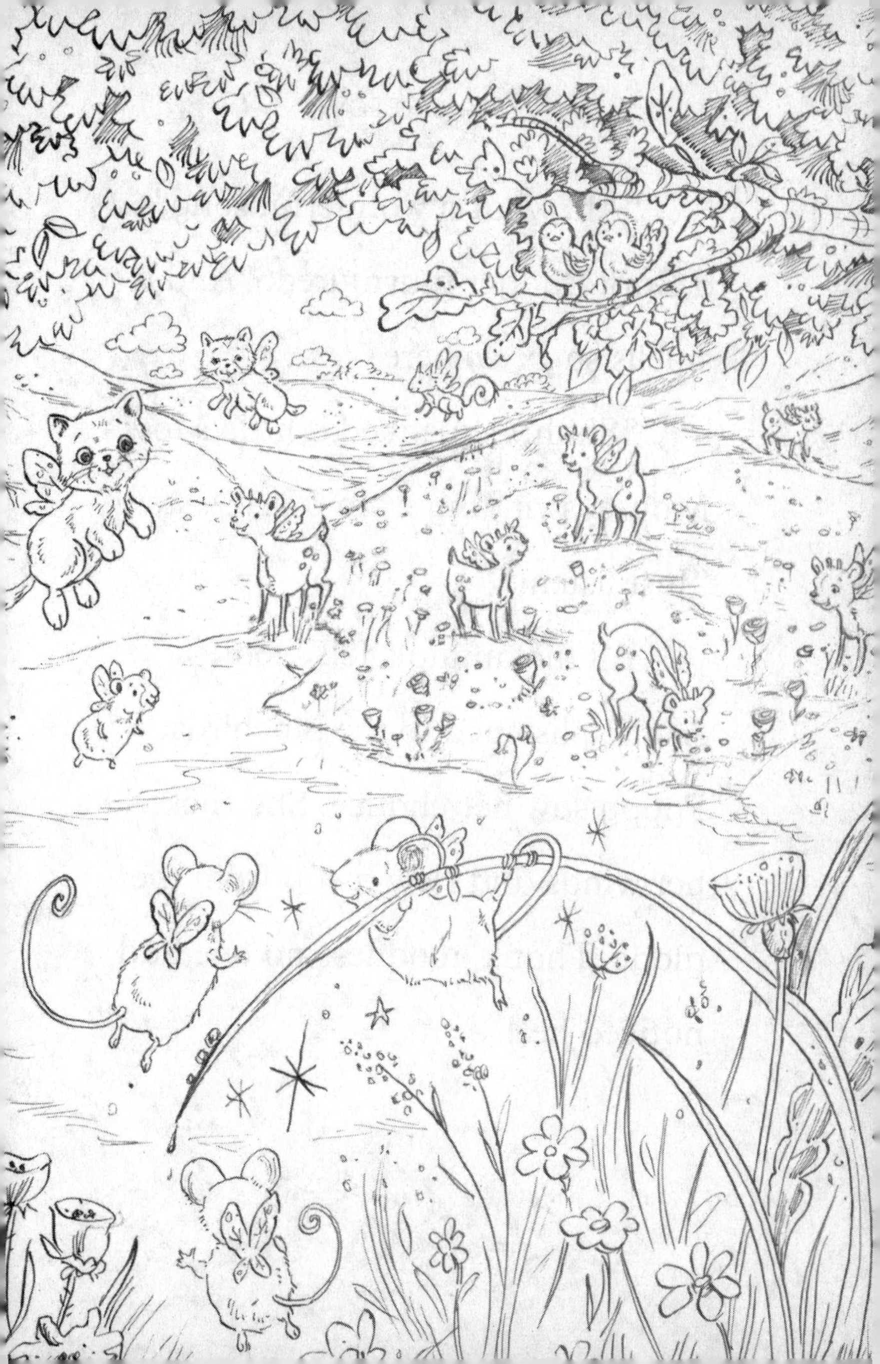

"Ah, what a wonderful song," a Bark Badger murmured. "And it smells so *lovely* here."

"Shhh," squeaked a little Moss Mouse, swinging from a grass stem. "Just listen!"

All the animals fell silent. As they listened to the bluebirds, Poppy saw her chance. She flicked her wings and flew away from the glade. Thank goodness no one had noticed her!

Poppy flew swiftly through the wood. She was just beginning to feel tired when she saw a gnarled old tree with juicy golden pears hanging from its branches. It had been a long time since breakfast and she was feeling very hungry, so she swooped down and landed under the tree.

She was just about to take a bite from one of the fallen pears when she heard a voice from above.

"Help!" the voice squeaked.

Poppy froze. Someone was in the tree and they were calling to her! But what was she going to do?

48

CHAPTER THREE

Poppy to the Rescue!

Everything went quiet. Poppy
was just wondering whether she'd
imagined the voice when she heard
it again.

"Help!" it cried. "Please help me!"

Poppy was puzzled. She hadn't seen anyone at all when she flew over the pear tree.

"Who are you?" she tried to say, but her voice wasn't working again and all that came out was "*Hm-hm-hm?*"

"I'm stuck!" the voice whimpered. "Please help me."

Whoever it was sounded very scared.

Poppy peered up. A tiny Cobweb Kitten, with fur the color of chocolate, was clinging to a high branch.

"Please! I want to get down," the kitten meowed, letting go of the branch and waving her paws at Poppy.

Poppy was amazed. The kitten wasn't holding on—so why hadn't she fallen out of the tree? Then Poppy saw that one of the kitten's golden wings was trapped.

Poppy felt so sorry for the kitten that she forgot all about being shy. "You poor thing," she

52

neighed. "Of course I'll help you get down."

"Oh, thank you!"

"What's your name? And how did you get stuck up there?" Poppy called. Her voice was working perfectly now—she didn't even have to think about it.

The kitten was trembling. "My name's Coco," she meowed. "What's yours?"

"Poppy," Poppy replied.

"Hello, Poppy. I was just on my way to meet my friends for a picnic when I spotted these juicy pears."

Poppy nodded. "They do look delicious."

"I thought they'd be perfect for the picnic," Coco said. "I swooped down to pick one, but then my wing got caught."

Poppy tossed her white mane. Then, with a swirl of her shimmering wings, she flew up

to the branch. But as soon as she landed, Poppy realized she couldn't reach Coco with her nose. There were too many twigs and leaves in the way.

"Please be quick!" Coco pleaded. "My wing is getting sore."

Carefully, Poppy turned and twirled her tail over Coco's wing, twisting it gently until it came free.

Coco leaped off the branch . . . then squealed with fright.

Poppy saw Coco tumbling down! She flapped her wings hard and flew after her. When she was close enough, she flicked out her tail as far as it would go and managed to catch Coco just before she hit the ground.

"Thank you so much!" Coco gasped as Poppy lowered her onto the grass. "My wing isn't working properly. I can't fly."

A tear welled in Coco's eye.

"And if I can't fly, I'll never get to the picnic in time."

The little kitten looked so sad that Poppy didn't stop to think. "I could take you there if you like," she said in a very soft voice.

Coco was so pleased she jumped up and down. "Ouch!" she squeaked as she tried to flutter her wings. "I must remember not to do that. Thank you, Poppy!"

"You're welcome," Poppy said.

Coco was being so bouncy it made Poppy feel shy again, so she didn't say anything else. She wrapped her tail around the kitten and lifted her onto her back.

"Ooh, this is so much fun!" Coco meowed, holding on to Poppy's coat with her paws. "I've always wondered what it must be like to be a Petal Pony—to gallop so fast and fly so high. Now I'm going to find out!"

59

Poppy tossed her head. She couldn't help feeling a little bit proud that Coco might want to be like her. "Let's go!" she neighed.

Coco told Poppy that the picnic was happening near Dewdrop Spring. Poppy set off through the trees at a smooth trot. Soon they came out into Honeydew Meadow.

"Could we go a bit faster?" asked Coco.

"Are you sure?" Poppy said.

"I don't want you to fall off."

"I'll hold on tight, I promise,"

Coco said.

Poppy stretched out her neck

and began to race across the golden flowers.

"Wheeee!" Coco squealed as Poppy leaped over a fallen log. "Woo-hooo!" she whooped as Poppy kicked up her heels and jumped over a hedge.

Poppy's hooves thundered across the golden meadow. When she couldn't gallop any faster, she unfurled her wings and soared into the air.

"Oooooh!" Coco meowed.

Poppy felt the little kitten clinging to her mane as they floated high over a hill where lots of green bushes grew.

"Those are the Mulberry Bushes," Poppy said. "That's where the Misty Wood Rabbit Warren is."

"We're nearly there, then!" squeaked Coco. "Dewdrop Spring runs right by the rabbit warren. Look, there are my friends!"

Poppy glanced down. She could see the silvery thread of Dewdrop Spring winding its way past the warren. Then she saw three fairy animals spreading out a picnic blanket made of moss on the banks of the spring. There was a Bud Bunny, a Moss Mouse, and a Holly Hamster.

Poppy's wings began to tremble. It was okay being with Coco. It was easy talking to just

one little kitten. But what would happen if she had to meet three new fairy animals all at once?

CHAPTER FOUR

Picnic Time!

Poppy's heart pounded as she
glided toward Dewdrop Spring.

"Hey—look at meeee!" Coco
called to her friends down below.

The three fairy animals were very surprised indeed when they looked up and saw Coco on Poppy's back.

"How did you get to ride on a Petal Pony?" squeaked the Moss Mouse.

"That looks like fun!" chuckled the Bud Bunny.

"Come down and start the picnic! I'm starving!" shouted the Holly Hamster, rubbing his furry tummy.

Poppy's blue wings glimmered as she circled in the air, looking for somewhere to land. She felt very shy with all of Coco's friends watching her.

Next to the picnic spot there was a grassy bank covered with bright yellow buttercups. Poppy fluttered down toward it.

"I'll drop you here, Coco," she whinnied. As soon as her hooves touched the ground, she carefully

lifted Coco down with her tail.

"I've got to go now," she explained hurriedly. "I've got loads of work to do and—"

But it was too late.

The Bud Bunny came hopping toward them through the buttercups. "Coco—who's your friend?" she asked.

Poppy hid her face in her mane. If only she'd flown away more quickly!

Then the Moss Mouse scampered up, his long whiskers twitching. "Are you all right, Coco?"

"I got stuck in a tree!" Coco explained. "I was trying to pick some pears for our picnic, but my wing got caught. It was horrible." Coco's tail fluffed up like a feather duster at the thought.

"That sounds awful. Oh, look, here comes hungry Harry!" said

the bunny as the Holly Hamster
trotted up on his chubby little legs.

"Who said pears? Did you say
pears?" he said to Coco, puffing
out his cheeks. "I love pears. Did
you bring some?"

Coco shook her head. "No, I was too scared to pick any. I thought I'd be stuck up there forever."

"How did you escape?" asked the mouse.

"Poppy rescued me," Coco purred. "She's amazing!" The kitten twined herself around Poppy's legs, rubbing them with her soft fur as she told her friends how the pony had freed her from the tree.

Coco's friends all looked at Poppy in admiration.

"I'm Max," squeaked the Moss Mouse, standing as tall as he could on his back legs and twirling his whiskers at Poppy.

"I'm Bobbi," said the Bud Bunny, twitching her velvety pink nose.

"And I'm hungry—*starving* hungry!" said Harry.

Poppy looked down at the

75

buttercups and tried to pretend that she wasn't really there. Her heart was beating so fast, and she felt too hot. If only they would all stop staring at her!

Harry looked longingly over at the picnic blanket. "Let's eat before my tummy gets so empty it starts to cry!" he groaned.

They all turned to the picnic. Poppy was relieved. Finally, she had a chance to escape. She spread

her wings, ready to take off. But just then, Max looked back.

"Don't go!" he cried when he saw her.

Poppy opened her mouth and tried to speak, but all that came out was, "*Hm-hm-hm!*"

Coco padded over and rubbed against Poppy's legs again. "You must come to our picnic," she purred.

"Please stay, Poppy!" Bobbi said.

"If you don't all hurry up, I am going to faint from starvation!" Harry called, sucking his cheeks in as thin as they would go—which wasn't very thin at all.

It was no good. Poppy's voice had disappeared again, and she didn't want to seem rude. All she could do was fold her wings back down and trot after the others to the picnic spot.

The mossy blanket was covered

with conker-shell bowls full of nuts
and seeds, bunches of tasty carrots
with leafy green tops, and a basket
of beautiful rosy apples.

Coco, Bobbi, Max, and Harry
settled down and started eating.
But Poppy felt much too shy to
sit down with them. So she stood
behind, shifting nervously from
hoof to hoof. She was very glad
that they were all too busy enjoying
the food to notice her.

If I went back to the buttercup patch, she thought, *I could wave my tail over the flowers to spread the perfume. Everyone would be happy, and they'd forget all about me.*

She was just about to slip away when Coco looked around. "Would you like an apple?" she asked.

Before Poppy could even try to answer, the little kitten came padding over with a shiny red

apple in her mouth. She put it

down in front of Poppy.

Poppy licked the apple, but

she didn't bite into it. If she made

a loud crunching noise, everyone would look at her again.

"Oooh!" squealed Coco suddenly. "What was that?" She wiped at her head with her paw.

Poppy felt a fat drop of water plop onto her mane.

Everyone looked up. The sun had disappeared, and a big black cloud was filling up the sky. It was starting to rain!

"Oh no!" squeaked Max,

holding a carrot over his head as
the drops began falling thick and
fast. "Our picnic will be ruined!"

CHAPTER FIVE

Under the Oak Tree

"I'm getting wet," meowed Coco,

shaking raindrops out of her fur.

"Me too," squeaked Max.

"We'd better get out of here."

"Never mind about getting wet—what about the food?" Harry cried. He started scampering about, gathering all the food in the middle of the mossy blanket. Then he folded the corners together and tied them tightly in a knot.

"Where can we go?" asked Bobbi, flicking the rain from her floppy ears. "There's no shelter here."

The rain was coming down

really hard now. *At least it will make the flowers grow*, Poppy thought. But she felt very sorry for the four friends. Their picnic was spoiled and they were going to get soaked. If she was brave enough, maybe she could help . . .

She took a deep breath. "Jump on my back!" she whinnied. As soon as the words burst from her mouth, she felt so shy she had to look down at her hooves.

"Really, Poppy?" said Bobbi, her eyes shining.

"Come on, quick!" said Coco, scampering up Poppy's tail and onto her back.

Bobbi did a giant hop and landed just behind Coco.

Harry and Max fluttered their little wings and floated up to join the others. "Don't forget the food!" Harry shrieked.

"I won't," Poppy said. "Hold

on tight!" She picked up the blanket
bundle with her mouth and started
cantering away from Dewdrop
Spring.

"Wheeee!" squealed Coco.

"Isn't this fun?"

"Bouncing bunnies!" cried

Bobbi. "It's brilliant!"

Poppy's tail streamed behind her as she galloped toward the trees. She knew just where to go. Right in the heart of the wood grew a tall oak tree with wide, leafy branches big enough to cover them all.

As soon as she spotted the tree, she slowed down to a gentle trot.

"This is perfect! We'll be dry here," squeaked Max as Poppy came to a halt.

Poppy carefully placed the blanket of food on the ground under the tree. Max and Harry fluttered down, and Bobbi and Coco both reached the ground in one big leap.

"Thank you, Poppy," said Harry as he untied the blanket with his front teeth. "I was saving the biggest apple for me, but you can have it. You deserve it!"

This time, Poppy was so glad

Coco's friends were happy that she didn't feel shy or embarrassed. She just took a bite out of the juicy apple and kept on crunching until it was all gone. When she'd finished, she noticed that Coco had disappeared.

"Where's Coco?" she asked.

"I'm here!" purred Coco, scampering up to Poppy with a bunch of daisies. "Lie down, Poppy, and shut your eyes—I'm

going to give you a wonderful
surprise."

Poppy lay down with her legs
folded underneath her. She closed
her eyes. She could feel Coco
playing with her mane—it was
lovely. Her whole body relaxed.

Finally, Coco tapped Poppy
on the nose. "Okay—ready!"

When Poppy opened her eyes,
she saw that Coco had woven a
daisy chain into her mane. The

little flowers looked like yellow and

white jewels.

"Thank you!" she whinnied.

"It's so pretty!"

"Thank *you*," replied Coco.

"You saved us from getting soaking wet. That rain is heavy—listen."

Poppy pricked her ears. *Pit-a-pat, pit-a-pat* went the raindrops as they sploshed on the leaves of the oak tree.

Suddenly, there was a loud *CRACK!* from high up in the sky.

"Uh-oh!" Bobbi cried. "A thunderstorm!"

"Help!" squealed Harry. He covered his ears with his paws.

95

"I'm scared," whispered Max as another *CRACK!* echoed through the sky.

"It's all right," said Poppy. "Hide under my mane, you two little ones. You'll be safe there."

"Wh-wh-what about all the f-f-f-food?" Harry stammered as he and Max snuggled under Poppy's mane. "What if it gets struck by lightning?"

"It won't," Poppy said calmly

as she gathered the remains of the
picnic toward her with her tail.
Coco and Bobbi cuddled up next to
her tummy. Poppy felt very brave
and strong as she swooshed her
tail around to hug them close.

BOOM! went the thunder.
Poppy could feel Max and Harry
trembling. Coco and Bobbi were
shivering, too. What could she do
to make them forget about the
thunder? Then she had an idea.

She'd have to be very brave indeed,

but maybe it would work. . . .

Poppy took a deep breath.

"Shall I tell you a story?" she

asked. She gave a small sigh of
relief. Her voice was still working!

"Yes, please!" said Bobbi.

Poppy cleared her throat.
"Once upon a time," she began in
a strong, clear voice, "there was a
baby Petal Pony called Pearl. Her
legs were so wobbly she couldn't
stand up."

"Why were they wobbly?"
asked Max.

"Because she was only one

99

hour old, and she hadn't learned
how to walk yet," said Poppy.
"It's quite hard to get the hang of
walking when your legs are as long
as a Petal Pony's."

"I'd be very scared if that was
me," Harry said.

"Pearl wasn't *too* scared,
because her mom was with her,"
Poppy said, "and her mom was
very nice and kind. 'Come on,
Pearl—you can do it,' her mom

100

said. So Pearl put her front hooves on the ground and pushed until she was halfway up, and . . ."

BOOM! went the thunder. All the animals cowered back against Poppy.

"What happened next?" Coco asked in a shaky voice.

"Pearl pushed and pushed with her hooves, but her legs were still too wobbly. Bump—down she fell again," said Poppy.

"Poor little Pearl," said Bobbi. "I hope there's a happy ending for her."

"So do I!" said a gruff voice, and a Bark Badger pushed his stripy face through the bushes.

Then a graceful Dream Deer stepped out from behind the tree. "I'm sure there is," she said in a soft, soothing voice. "But we'll have to hear the rest of the story to find out. . . ."

Now there were rustling noises from all around. Lots of fairy animals were coming under the oak tree to take shelter from the rain. There were Stardust Squirrels and Hedgerow Hedgehogs, Bud Bunnies and Pollen Puppies—and they were all looking at Poppy and waiting for her to continue her story.

There were so many of them that Poppy began to feel a little

POPPY THE PONY

shy again. What would she do if her voice stopped working and she couldn't tell the rest of the story?

She spotted a patch of pansies growing from the roots of the oak tree. She swished her tail softly over the purple flowers, and a soothing perfume drifted out.

"Mmm!" sighed Max as he climbed out from under Poppy's mane. "That smells nice. I'm not a bit frightened of the thunder now."

105

All the fairy animals who had gathered around were looking calm and happy, too.

Poppy went on. "Pearl's mom said: 'Come on, Pearl, you can do it,' and she nudged Pearl with her nose. 'I can't!' said Pearl. 'My legs won't work!' 'They will,' said Pearl's mom. 'You've just got to believe.'"

Poppy paused for a moment. She looked around at all the animals. Their eyes shone as they

106

waited to hear what happened next to baby Pearl. They'd forgotten all about the thunderstorm.

"Pearl stretched out her front legs," Poppy continued. "'I *can* stand up!' she said, and she pushed and she pushed until she was almost up, but then her legs started wobbling again. . . ."

A whisper went up from the animals: "*Come on, baby Pearl! You can do it!*"

"Pearl's mom reached out with her nose and she pushed against Pearl's tail so she didn't fall over again—and suddenly, Pearl was standing up!"

"Hooray!" cried the animals.

"Baby Pearl took one wobbly step, and then she took another. Then Pearl's mom trotted away!"

"No!" squeaked Max. "What did Pearl do?"

Poppy smiled at him and

carried on with the story. "'Don't go without me!' Pearl whinnied. And suddenly she found that her legs were working! Faster and faster they went—until she was galloping after her mom! 'I *can* do it!' Pearl neighed as she cantered along at her mom's side. 'Yes, you can,' her mom said. 'And one day, you'll be the fastest Petal Pony in Misty Wood.' The end!" said Poppy.

"Yay!" A big cheer went up from all the animals.

They liked her story! Poppy tossed her head and flicked her long mane with its pretty daisy chain.

110

And the strangest thing
was that although everyone was
looking at her, Poppy didn't feel the
slightest bit shy.

CHAPTER SIX

Surprise!

Max fluttered his wings and flew beside Poppy's head. "Was that story really about you?" he whispered.

"Yes," Poppy whispered back. "My mom helped me to stand up

when I was a baby. And one day, maybe I'll be the fastest pony in Misty Wood!"

"I bet you will," said Max.

"The rain's stopped," said Coco, looking up at the top of the oak tree. "The storm's over!" The little Cobweb Kitten fluttered her wings and flew back and forth over the ferns. "My wing's healed!" she called. "Your story made me feel better, Poppy!"

Poppy swished her tail and neighed happily. Lots of other animals started coming over to talk to her. Poppy jumped to her feet, but there was nothing to be shy about. Everyone just wanted to be friendly.

"Your mane would make a great bark pattern," said one of the Bark Badgers. "Come and pose for us sometime. Maybe you could tell us another story—and make

114

everything smell lovely and sweet again?"

"Come around and visit us for snacks!" said a Stardust Squirrel. "We've got some tasty hazelnuts!"

"Hazelnuts? Who said hazelnuts?" Harry cried.

"*Woof! Woof!*" barked a Pollen Puppy. "How about a game of chase? Whenever you like, we'll be ready! *Woof!*"

A Dream Deer blinked shyly

at Poppy. "Would you like to come running through the woods with us?" she murmured. "You could spread the flower smells and tell us a story while we go!"

Max's whiskers were twitching again. "I was just thinking," he squeaked. "You might be tired after all that running around and storytelling. Drop by my burrow and we'll make you a big comfy moss cushion to lie on."

"I would love that! Thank you," said Poppy.

Golden shafts of sunlight were shimmering through the branches now. The leaves and ferns of Misty Wood looked so fresh and green. All that was missing was the sweet smell of flowers. The rain had washed it away! It was time for Poppy to get going.

"I'll come and visit you all," Poppy said to her new friends. "And

we'll have loads of fun. But first I've got my special job to do. Good-bye for now—and I'll see all of you very soon!"

As the fairy animals called their good-byes, Poppy twirled her blue wings and floated away through the trees. The leafy branches were covered in dazzling raindrops that glinted in the sunlight, and a rainbow twinkled softly in the sky.

Poppy glided down and swished her tail over the bluebells and buttercups, roses and lilies, until Misty Wood was filled with the sweetest smells once again. Finally, as the sky was turning pink and the sun began to fade, she galloped back to Sundown Hill.

Her mom was waiting for her, looking worried. "There you are, Poppy!" she neighed. "Did you get caught in the rain?"

Poppy blew on her mom's nose to say hello. "I was fine," she said. "The thunder was very loud, though."

"It was," Poppy's mom said with a shiver. "I was worried about you, all on your own in the storm."

Poppy was about to explain what had happened when there was a flicker of wings close by. It was Max!

"Hello, Poppy," he squeaked as

he fluttered past. "Don't forget to come and get your pony-sized moss cushion!"

Poppy's mom's eyes opened wide with surprise, but before she could say anything, a Bark Badger came trundling through the grass.

"See you soon!" he called to Poppy. "Drop by anytime!"

"Poppy! What's going on?" asked her mom.

Poppy was just about to answer

when a Dream Deer strolled past. "Can't wait to go running with you!" the deer called softly.

Then a Pollen Puppy bounced up. "See you soon for our game of chase," he yelped, and then scampered away.

"Well!" Poppy's mom said with a smile. "You *have* been busy, Poppy. Very busy indeed!" She nuzzled Poppy's neck. "And what's this lovely daisy chain doing in your mane?"

Poppy felt her heart swell as
she thought of all the fairy animals
she had met that day. Her first-ever
friends! There was no need to be
shy after all.

"A *friend* made it for me!"
Poppy told her mom, who looked as
pleased as Poppy felt.

Then Poppy kicked up her
heels, neighed with joy, and
cantered off to find a tasty patch of
grass for her supper.

125

Turn the page for

lots of fun

Misty Wood

activities!

Picnic Time!

In the story, Poppy's new friends have a delicious picnic with lots of tasty treats for everyone.

What are your favorite things to eat at a picnic? Write them down on the next page.

1. ....

2. ....

3. ....

4. ....

5. ....

6. ....

7. ....

8. ....

Draw the treats from your list on page 129 on the picnic blanket.

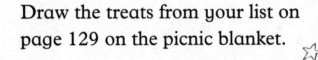

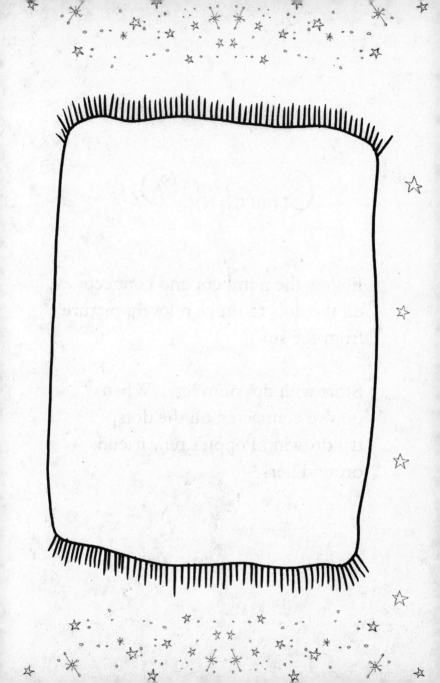

Connect the Dots

Follow the numbers and connect
all the dots to make a lovely picture
from the story.

Start with dot number 1. When
you've connected all the dots,
try drawing Poppy's new friends
around her!

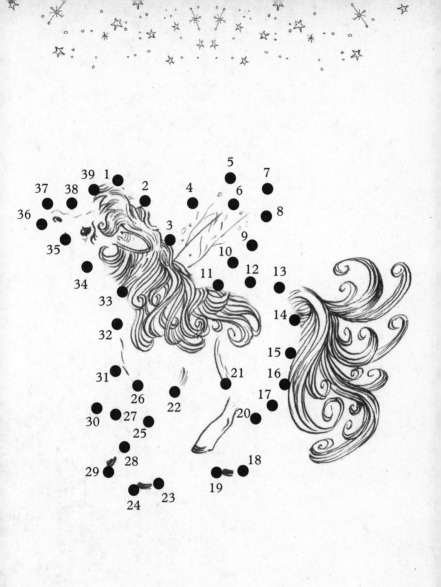

Fairy Animals
of Misty Wood

Hailey the Hedgehog

Lily Small

Henry Holt and Company
New York

With special thanks to Liss Norton

Henry Holt and Company
Publishers since 1866
175 Fifth Avenue
New York, New York 10010
mackids.com

First published in the United States in 2016 by Henry Holt and Company.
Originally published in Great Britain in 2013 by Egmont UK Limited.

Library of Congress Cataloging-in-Publication Data is available.
Paper Over Board ISBN 978-1-250-11398-6
Paperback ISBN 978-1-250-11399-3

Our books may be purchased in bulk for promotional, educational, or business use.
Please contact your local bookseller or the Macmillan Corporate
and Premium Sales Department at (800) 221-7945 ext. 5442
or by e-mail at MacmillanSpecialMarkets@macmillan.com.

First American Edition—2016
Printed in the United States of America by
LSC Communications, Harrisonburg, Virginia

Hardcover
1 3 5 7 9 10 8 6 4 2

Paperback
5 7 9 10 8 6 4

Contents

CHAPTER ONE

Parade Day!

Winter had come to Misty Wood, and the fairy animals were very excited—today was the day of the Christmas Parade!

1

Hailey, a tiny hedgehog, lay in her cozy bed of moss, listening to the wind outside singing through the trees. She pulled her blanket of velvety dock leaves up to her nose.

"I do love winter," Hailey said with a sigh. As she pictured the wind blowing the last of the golden leaves from the branches and the woods twinkling with frost, she started to smile.

"Are you up, Hailey?" her dad

called from the far end of their
burrow.

"Nearly," Hailey called back.
She jumped out of bed, licked her
tiny pink paws, and gave her face
a quick wash. Then she checked her
dandelion clock. "Yay!" she cried.
"It's breakfast time!"

When she got to the other
end of the burrow, her dad was
busy chopping acorns. "Morning,
Hailey," he said. "I'm making

3

you some acorn porridge to keep
you nice and warm out there. The
woods are going to need a lot of
tidying up before the parade."

"Great!" Hailey exclaimed. "I
love having lots of leaves to collect."
She fluttered her silver-and-red
wings excitedly, sending sparkles of
glittering light around the burrow.

Hailey was a Hedgerow
Hedgehog. Like all the other fairy
animals, she had a special job

to do to help make Misty Wood
a wonderful place to live. The
Hedgerow Hedgehogs' job was to
collect fallen leaves on their prickly
spines, to keep the woods neat
and tidy. That was why Hailey
loved winter so much. There were
so many colorful leaves to gather,
especially on a windy day like this.

Dad finished making the
porridge and poured it into three
nutshell bowls. Hailey took hers

and went to sit on a pebble stool in
the corner. Just as she ate her first
mouthful, a gust of cold air came
whisking through the burrow.

"It's only me," a voice called.
Hailey's mom hurried inside. Her
paws were full of mistletoe sprigs.
"Goodness!" she exclaimed. "What
a wind!" Laying the mistletoe on
the conker table, she smoothed
down the ruffled fur on her face
and legs.

7

"Ooh, is the mistletoe for the Christmas Parade?" Hailey asked. She could hardly wait for the parade to start. It took place every year. All the fairy animals dressed up in beautiful leaves and berries and marched through Misty Wood behind the Moss Mouse pipe-and-drum band. Afterward, everyone visited the nests and burrows of their friends to admire their decorations and to share a tasty

nibble or an acorn cup of warm
cranberry juice.

"Yes," her mom replied. "I'm
using mistletoe and holly this year."
She turned around, and Hailey saw
that her mom's prickles were stuck
all over with shiny red holly berries.

"I'll string them together
to make garlands," her mom
continued. She shook the berries
from her spines and pushed them
into a tidy pile beside the fire.

9

Hailey couldn't stop smiling as she pictured herself wearing a beautiful red-and-white garland. In fact, she was grinning so much that some porridge trickled out of the corner of her mouth! Hailey quickly

licked it up with her velvety pink tongue.

"Here's your breakfast," said Hailey's dad, passing her mom a bowl of porridge. "And I'm making my special chestnut pudding for after the parade."

"Yippee!" Hailey cheered. That was another good thing about winter—there were always chestnuts to be found, and Dad's chestnut pudding was *delicious*!

11

Hailey ate her porridge quickly. Every day she made sure that Misty Wood was spick-and-span, but today—parade day—she was determined to be extra careful. Today, she wouldn't leave a single leaf out of place. And she had to make sure she got home earlier than usual, too, so she'd have time to dress up.

"I'm off, then," she said as soon as her bowl was empty.

"Don't forget that the parade begins at one o'clock, Hailey," her mom reminded her.

"I won't," Hailey said with a smile. There was *no way* she was going to miss her favorite event!

Spreading her wings, she fluttered up the long passageway that led out of her warm burrow and into Hawthorn Hedgerows, which grew at the very edge of Misty Wood.

As soon as Hailey got above ground she could see that the wind had been busy. Only a few leaves still clung to the twigs above her head. They fluttered as the wind danced around them, whistling its winter tune.

They'll be off soon, too, thought Hailey, smiling. *And then I'll have even more leaves to tidy.*

She flitted out from under the hedgerow and gasped in delight.

14

Jack Frost had been at work during the night, sprinkling his glittering ice crystals across the grass. The crystals shimmered pink, blue, and silver in the wintry sunshine, and each blade of grass stood up stiff and straight no matter how hard the wind blew.

Hailey gazed around. "*Beautiful*," she breathed. She fluttered up into the air and spread her wings wide so the wind would lift her high. She

15

wanted to look at the grassy spaces
between the hedgerows. "I'll start
collecting leaves in the messiest
patch," she said to herself.

Up, up, up she soared into
the clear blue sky. Soon, Misty

16

Wood was spread out beneath her

like a colorful patchwork quilt.

The frosted grass glinted silver.

Dewdrop Spring was the same

bright blue as the sky, with spots of

shiny ice here and there. And the

patch of snowdrops beside it looked as clean and white as a fluffy cloud.

Farther on still, Moonshine Pond shone pearly blue, full of glowing moonbeams, and beyond that was the pretty, vivid purple of Heather Hill.

Right in the center of it all was a patch of deep, dark green—the mysterious Heart of Misty Wood, where the Wise Wishing Owl lived.

Hailey had never seen the Wise Wishing Owl, but she had heard lots of stories about her wisdom. And everyone said that she had the power to grant wishes.

As Hailey looked around, she spotted a patch of leaf-strewn grass not far from her burrow. She quickly fluttered down. "Perfect!" she cried happily, puffing out her spikes. "Now I'm ready to start work!"

CHAPTER TWO

Hungry Hugo!

Tucking her nose and legs in
against her tummy and folding
her glittering wings, Hailey curled
herself into a tight ball. Then she

rolled to and fro across the frosty

grass, gathering the leaves on her

prickles.

Soon the patch of grass was

clear. Hailey scurried over to a

21

nearby hedge and shook herself.
The leaves fluttered down from
her spines, and she scooped them
into a tidy heap at the base of the
hedge. Smiling, she looked across
the spotless grass. "Good job!" she
congratulated herself. "Now on to
the next one."

She unfurled her wings and
flew farther into the woods.

Soon, she came to a grove
where the Holly Hamsters were

22

hard at work. They were nibbling
the glossy holly leaves into their
beautiful curved shapes.

"Hello, Holly Hamsters!"
Hailey called as she fluttered past.

"Hello, Hailey!" they called
back, their chubby cheeks bulging.

Just beyond the holly grove
was an ancient chestnut tree with
twisted branches and a huge,
fat trunk. Leaves were scattered
around it, and Hailey eagerly

swooped down to gather them
all up.

As she rolled to and fro,
collecting the leaves, she made
up a little song:

> *I love winter when the wild wind*
>
> *blows,*
>
> *Scattering the leaves all around,*
>
> *all around,*
>
> *Even though it chills my nose*
>
> *and toes,*
>
> *When I roll on the frosty ground.*

Suddenly, she heard a small voice. "I hate winter," it said. "I don't know why you're singing about it. It's the worst season of the whole year!"

Hailey stopped rolling and uncurled herself. She looked around in surprise. How could anybody hate winter?

A teeny-tiny Holly Hamster with pale brown fur and yellow wings was crouched on the edge of

25

the holly grove. His head and wings were drooping miserably. Hailey recognized him—it was Hugo.

"Whatever's the matter, Hugo?" asked Hailey.

"I've ruined my holly bush," he replied, looking up sadly. "And now it's going to look horrible for the Christmas Parade. Every fairy animal in the whole wood will march past here and see what I've done."

Hailey fluttered over to him.

26

"Perhaps it's not as bad as you . . ."
She fell silent as she spotted the
bush. "Oh, dear."

The bush was almost
completely bare, with every leaf
nibbled right down to the stem.

Hailey stared at Hugo. "What happened to it?"

"I was hungry," Hugo said. "And the leaves were so yummy I couldn't stop eating them." He peered up at Hailey dreamily. "Honestly, they were the most delicious things I've ever tasted—even more delicious than chestnuts!" He sat back on the ground and gave a loud burp.

Hailey's tummy rumbled as

28

she thought of her dad's chestnut pudding. It was hard to imagine anything tasting nicer. They must have been very tasty leaves indeed!

"Maybe I should try digging up the whole bush," Hugo said. "Then I could hide it." The tiny hamster leaped up and began scratching at the soil around the bush's roots.

"No, Hugo!" Hailey cried. "Don't do that." She rubbed her

29

nose thoughtfully. "I think I know what to do," she said at last.

Hugo looked at her hopefully, his dark eyes shining. "Really?"

"Wait here a moment," said Hailey. She fluttered back to the chestnut tree and quickly rolled over the last of the leaves to stick them to her prickles. Then she whooshed back to Hugo.

"Here you go," she said, shaking the leaves to the ground.

"You can nibble these into holly leaf shapes, and I'll hang them on the bush."

Hugo bounced up and down on his hind legs. "That's brilliant! Thanks, Hailey!" he cried.

"Just make sure you don't gobble them all up this time," Hailey said with a grin.

"I won't," Hugo said, patting his furry tummy. "I'm far too full!" Then he set to work, taking dainty

little bites out of the edges of the bright chestnut tree leaves.

Hailey twisted the leaf stems around the holly twigs and soon the bush was covered in golden holly-shaped leaves.

"These leaves make my bush look so pretty!" Hugo cried out happily. He hugged Hailey, then leaped back. "Ouch! I forgot all about your prickles!" He chuckled, rubbing his paws.

"Sorry," giggled Hailey. "But I'm glad you're pleased with your *holly* bush."

"I am!" Hugo exclaimed. Then he looked at the little pile of spare leaves next to him. "Can you close

your eyes for a minute?" he asked Hailey.

"Why?" Hailey said, puzzled.

"I can't tell you yet—it's a surprise."

Hailey loved surprises. She closed her eyes and listened, trying to work out what Hugo was doing. But all she could hear was the rustle of leaves.

"Ta-da!" cried Hugo after a few minutes.

Hailey opened her eyes.

"I made this just for you," Hugo said. He held up a beautiful garland made from all the spare leaves. He slipped it over Hailey's head. "It's to say thank you for helping me."

"It's lovely!" Hailey exclaimed. "Thanks, Hugo. I'll wear it in the Christmas Parade. Ooh, I'd better get going—I've got loads of work to do before then!"

CHAPTER THREE

A Shimmer of Moonbeams

Hailey soared into the air and
fluttered quickly over the rabbit
warren. Down below, her friend

Bella the Bud Bunny was hard at work opening snowdrop buds with her twitchy nose. Hailey waved, but she didn't fly down to speak to Bella in case it made her late for the parade.

She flew over Dewdrop Spring, then on to Moonshine Pond, which shone like a blue pearl in the winter sunshine. "Ha!" she cried as she spotted some leaves at the pond's edge.

Hailey flew down to land. She curled into a ball and rolled quickly down the bank, gathering the leaves on her prickles as she went. She sang her song as she rolled faster and faster:

39

I love winter when the wild wind

blows,

Scattering the leaves all around,

all around,

Even though it chills my nose

and toes,

When I roll on the frosty ground.

"I used to love winter, but I most definitely don't anymore!" said a gloomy voice.

The voice was coming from a tall pine tree beside the pond.

40

Hailey unrolled quickly, and looked around in surprise. "Who said that?" she asked.

"Me, Maisie the Moonbeam Mole," the voice replied softly.

Hailey was very puzzled indeed. Moonbeam Moles didn't usually come out during the day. They did their special job at nighttime— catching moonbeams and scattering them in Moonshine Pond to make it look pearly and beautiful. During

41

the day they stayed in their burrows and slept—and they certainly didn't go climbing trees! Hailey knew that they woke up specially for the Christmas Parade each year—but it was a bit too early yet.

Hailey fluttered over quickly to investigate.

A pair of tiny brown eyes peeked out from among the pine needles. They looked very tired and were full of tears.

"What's wrong, Maisie?" Hailey gasped. "And why are you still awake?"

"I've been here since last night." Maisie sniffed sadly. "My net's caught in this tree, and I can't pull it free." She crept along a branch and pointed up to the top of the tree with a trembling paw.

Hailey saw something glowing among the branches. It was the net—crammed full of twinkling

moonbeams. It had gotten tangled around some pinecones.

"I can't put my moonbeams into the pond"—Maisie gulped—"so it won't look lovely for the Christmas Parade."

"But it *does* look lovely," Hailey told her. "I noticed it when I was flying this way. It looks like a beautiful pearl." She flew up and patted the tiny mole's shoulder, trying to make her feel better.

45

"Not my bit of the pond," sobbed Maisie. She pointed to a patch of water close to the bank. Now Hailey understood why Maisie was so upset. The water there was dark and still, with not even a hint of glistening moonlight.

Hailey thought hard. "I know what to do!" she cried. "I'll hook my prickles through your net. Then I'll be able to fly up and lift it clear of those pinecones."

Maisie stopped crying and gazed hopefully at Hailey. "Do you think it will work?" she whispered.

"There's only one way to find out," said Hailey.

She soared to the top of the tree, then fluttered around it, hooking the net over her prickles. "Here goes," she called. Flapping her wings hard, she flew higher still. Part of the net came free and some pinecones dropped to the ground.

"It's working!" squealed Maisie happily.

Hailey flapped her wings harder than ever. More pinecones dropped down and now most of the net was free. "One more try," Hailey panted. Using all of her strength, she zoomed into the air and suddenly the net was dangling free below her. The moonbeams twinkled as they swung from side to side.

"Hurray!" Hailey cheered. She flew to the ground with the heavy net.

Maisie fluttered down beside her, her lilac wings shimmering in the sunshine. "Thank you, thank you," she cried. Her tiny eyes shone with relief as she unhooked the net from Hailey's spines. "Now the pond will look perfect for the parade!"

Scooping out a pawful of

moonbeams, Maisie tossed them into the patch of dark water. They plopped down out of sight, then rose to the surface and their beautiful pearly light rippled out, making the water gleam.

"That looks beautiful, Maisie," breathed Hailey, flying up to see the pond from above.

"All because of you," replied Maisie. She reached into her net and took out the last glowing

50

moonbeam. "May I give you a
present to thank you for helping
me?" she asked shyly.

"Oh yes, please!" Hailey cried. She loved presents!

Maisie placed the moonbeam on the biggest leaf in Hailey's garland. Hailey watched entranced as gold and silver sparkles spread from leaf to leaf. Soon the whole garland was twinkling brightly.

"Thank you!" gasped Hailey, astonished. She'd never seen anything so beautiful before. It was as though she were wearing

a necklace made of glittering

moonlight.

"No, thank *you*, Hailey,"

Maisie said. "If you hadn't helped

me, the pond wouldn't have looked

53

its best for the Christmas Parade today."

"The parade!" Hailey cried, remembering how much she had to do before it began. "I must go! Bye, Maisie."

CHAPTER FOUR

A Starry Surprise

Hailey fluttered up into the air and headed for the trees that grew in the Heart of Misty Wood. She could see a few untidy leaves on the grass

there. As she drew near, she started to sing her winter song:

I love winter when the wild wind

blows—

"Well, I don't!" boomed a cross voice. It was coming from behind a tree at the very back of the Heart of Misty Wood.

Hailey peeped around the tree trunk nervously, wondering who it could be.

Boris, one of the Bark Badgers,

was hunched on the frosty ground. He was frowning at his paw.

"What's wrong, Boris?" Hailey asked. The Bark Badgers carved beautiful patterns into tree trunks with their strong claws. They were usually very kind and helpful. Hailey had never seen one looking so grumpy before.

"I'm supposed to be carving wintry patterns into the bark of the trees around here," Boris replied.

57

"I wanted everything to be perfect for the parade, so I flew up onto a branch to reach farther up the trunk. But the branch was slippery with frost and I fell down." He held up his paw and Hailey saw that it was sore and swollen. "Now my paw's so painful that I can't do my job," he sighed.

"Poor you," Hailey said. She wondered what she could do to help him.

"I should have been more careful!" Boris said glumly. "Now when the parade comes past here, the fairy animals won't be thinking happy, Christmassy thoughts.

They'll be thinking, look at those plain old trees!"

Suddenly, they heard some loud barking and looked around, startled. A group of Pollen Puppies came scampering along, their ears flopping and their tongues hanging out with excitement. "Hey! Aren't you coming to the Christmas Parade?" the puppies woofed, wagging their tails and scattering specks of golden pollen all around.

"Is it time?" Hailey asked them anxiously.

"Nearly," one of the puppies woofed. "And we don't want to be late!"

"Neither do I!" Hailey gulped as the playful pups went bounding away. Her mind started whirring. She couldn't leave poor Boris looking so unhappy. Maybe she could help him *and* make it back home in time for the start of the parade. . . .

"Let me help," Hailey said. "My spines are nearly as sharp as a badger's claws. If you tell me what to do, perhaps I can carve the tree trunks for you."

Boris's face broke into a cheery smile. "That would be wonderful!" he exclaimed.

Hailey flew up and pressed her prickles against the first tree. "Okay, I'm ready," she said. "Tell me what to do."

"Go up a bit," called Boris.

Hailey fluttered upward. She felt her spines cutting through the tree's bark. "I think it's working!" she cried excitedly.

63

"Now right a bit," Boris said, beaming.

Hailey flew right.

"Left, then down," called Boris.

Hailey followed all of Boris's instructions.

"That's it," he said at last. "The first tree's finished. Let's see if it worked."

Hailey turned to look at the tree trunk. "Oh!" she gasped. "How pretty!" Her spines had carved a

pattern of beautiful lacy snowflakes cascading from the sky.

"Next tree!" declared Boris. "Quick!"

Hailey worked at top speed, and soon she'd carved snowflake patterns into all of Boris's trees. "I'd better go home now," she said as she turned to admire the last carved trunk.

"Hold on, there's just one more thing to do," said Boris, holding

up a piece of smooth bark that had been gnawed into a diamond shape. Hurriedly, Hailey pressed her spines against it and moved in the directions Boris told her.

"There," he said. "All done." He held up the bark to show Hailey and she saw that she'd carved a beautiful star.

"Lovely!" she exclaimed.

"It's for you," Boris said. "To thank you for all your help." He

hung it right in the middle of her

glowing leaf garland.

"Thank you!" cried Hailey.

"And now I must fly! Bye, Boris."

She made up her mind to go

straight home. "If I stop and pick

up any more leaves, I won't have time to get ready for the parade," she said to herself.

Her red-and-silver wings fluttered furiously as she sped along. She raced past a tree hung with balls of white-berried mistletoe. It reminded her of the decorations her mom was making, and she flapped her wings harder.

Just as she was approaching Dandelion Dell, she spotted some

leaves scattered messily on the ground beneath a large oak tree.

"Oh, dear!" Hailey squeaked. The parade would be coming this way, and everyone would see them. *I'll pick them up quickly*, she thought, *then I'll rush straight home. I should still be on time.*

Hurriedly, she flew down, then curled up tight and began to roll this way and that, gathering the leaves. As soon as she started doing

her job she stopped worrying about being late and started singing her wintry song again:

> *I love winter when the wild wind*
>> *blows,*
> *Scattering the leaves all around,*
>> *all around,*
> *Even though it chills my nose*
>> *and toes,*
> *When I roll on the frosty ground.*

"How can you sing at a time like this?" a voice called from a

branch in the tree high above her.

Hailey stopped singing and uncurled quickly. "A time like what?" she replied, fluttering upward.

"A time as terrible and horrible and awful as this!" the voice wailed.

CHAPTER FIVE

Acorn Disaster!

Hailey flew closer. A beautiful silver
Stardust Squirrel with cute tufty
ears was crouched miserably on a
branch, a broken basket beside her.

"Are you all right?" Hailey

asked anxiously.

"No," huffed the squirrel. "I

am actually all *wrong*!"

"Oh, dear." Hailey scratched her head with a tiny pink paw. "What's the matter?"

The squirrel sighed and twitched her bushy tail, sending a puff of glittery stardust into the air. "Are you sure you want to know?" she said, looking at Hailey and tilting her head to one side.

Hailey nodded.

"It's a very sad story. It's so sad it might even make you cry."

"Oh, er, that's all right," said Hailey bravely.

"Okay then." The squirrel clasped her front paws together. "Once upon a time, there was a very beautiful Stardust Squirrel called Sabrina—that's me," she added.

Hailey nodded and smiled.

"And one day—today, actually—Sabrina's mommy sent her out to fetch some acorns to decorate the delicious cake that

she's making for the Christmas Parade. So Sabrina did as she was told, because as well as being beautiful she's a very good little Stardust Squirrel. She filled her basket right to the brim. But then disaster struck!" Sabrina stared at her basket sadly. "Her basket broke and the acorns went all over the ground." Sabrina looked at Hailey. "Isn't that just the saddest story you've ever heard?"

Hailey nodded solemnly. "Yes, it is a very sad story," she said. "But maybe I can help you give it a happy ending."

Sabrina's eyes lit up. "How?"

Hailey fluttered over and examined the basket. It was woven from stems of dried grass, but some of them had broken and there was a hole in the bottom.

"Let's try putting some leaves over the hole," suggested Hailey.

"That might do the trick." She shook some leaves from her prickles, then carefully pressed a few on the bottom of the basket.

"Ooh, that looks a lot better," Sabrina said, twitching her tail

excitedly. "You can't see the hole at all now."

Hailey and Sabrina flew down to the ground. There were acorns scattered all over the grass, and they scampered around, picking them up and dropping them into the basket.

"Here goes," she said, lifting it.

For a moment it looked as though the repair was strong enough, but then the acorns and

leaves fell through the hole and
rolled across the grass again.

"Oh no!" Sabrina groaned.
"Now my story is going to have
an even sadder ending than it did
before!"

"Don't worry, I know how
we can definitely make it happy,"
Hailey said.

Sabrina frowned at her. "How?"

"I'll collect them with my
prickles. I'm sure they'll pick up

81

acorns just as well as they pick up leaves from the ground."

Sabrina looked doubtful. "There's an awful lot of them."

"Well, I've got an awful lot of prickles!" Hailey giggled. She curled into a ball and began to roll. Soon all the acorns were stuck to her prickles, along with the rest of the fallen leaves.

"Come on, let's get these to your mom," Hailey said. "We'll

have to hurry. The parade will be starting soon, and we mustn't miss it."

"Thank you!" Sabrina cried. "Now my story will have a very happy ending indeed!"

They flew at top speed through the trees, dodging between the branches. "There!" said Sabrina at last as a large nest came into view. It was made of sticks, dried grass, and leaves, and it was wedged into the fork where two branches joined

the trunk of a tall beech tree. They landed on a large branch.

"If you don't mind, I'll just put the acorns here," said Hailey. "I've got to go home to get ready."

"That will be great," Sabrina replied. "I can easily roll them into our nest from here."

Hailey shook her prickles. A few of the acorns came tumbling off, but most of them stayed put.

"Hang on, I'll get them off,"

said Sabrina. Grabbing an acorn, she pulled with all her might. "I'm not hurting you, am I, Hailey?"

Hailey could feel the tug on her spines but it wasn't sore. "No, it's okay, pull as hard as you can!"

Sabrina pulled and pulled and then, finally . . . *pop!* . . . the acorn came away from Hailey's spine.

"Hurray," cheered Hailey and Sabrina together.

"Now I *know* I'm strong

enough to get them off," said

Sabrina proudly. "I'll be as quick

as I can, so you're not late for the

parade." One by one, Sabrina

yanked the acorns from Hailey's

spines. "That's all of them!" she panted at last. "And a good thing, too. I'm puffed out!"

"Phew!" Hailey sighed with relief. "Now I must fly home as *fast* as my wings can take me!"

"Just a minute," Sabrina said as Hailey was about to flutter into the air. Sabrina flew above Hailey and flicked her tail. Twinkling silver stardust showered down on Hailey. "That's to say thank you

for helping me," Sabrina said with
a smile.

"Wow!" Hailey gasped,
twisting her head to look at her
spines. They were twinkling like
stars. "Thanks, Sabrina. That looks
amazing!" Hailey flew up into the
air. "See you at the parade," she
called as she sped off through the
trees. "If I get there in time . . ." she
whispered to herself.

CHAPTER SIX

An Unexpected Guest

Hailey flew faster than she'd ever
flown before. Misty Wood raced
by in a blur, but at last she saw
Hawthorn Hedgerows.

Zooming toward the ground,

she saw all the Hedgerow

Hedgehogs outside her burrow.

They were dressed in beautiful

garlands made of berries, acorns,
and golden leaves, ready for the
Christmas Parade.

Hailey's mom and dad were

among them, decked out in bright holly berries and mistletoe. They were looking around the crowd anxiously. Their eyes lit up in relief when they saw Hailey swishing through the air toward them.

"Where have you been?" Hailey's mom asked as she landed.

"Sorry," Hailey panted. "I had to help some friends and it made me late. Do I still have time to get dressed up for the parade?"

Suddenly, Hailey noticed that everyone was staring at her, their mouths gaping in astonishment. She began to feel a tiny bit worried.

"What's wrong?" she asked. She wondered if there was still an acorn or two stuck on her prickles.

"Nothing's wrong," her dad replied. "You look . . ."

"Wonderful!" her mom finished for him.

"Yes, you do," the other

hedgehogs agreed, crowding around to see her better.

Hailey's neighbors Henry and Hilda scurried into their burrow and came back carrying an upturned mushroom cap filled with water that they used as a mirror. "Here," they said, setting it down in front of Hailey. "Take a look at yourself."

Hailey peered at her reflection. "Oh!" she gasped. Looking back at her was a hedgehog whose fur

and prickles twinkled with silver stardust. Around her neck she wore a beautiful leafy garland that shone with pearly moonlight. A diamond-shaped piece of bark carved with a five-pointed star hung from it. Hailey stared and stared. She could hardly believe that the reflection was hers.

"That's the best Christmas costume I've ever seen!" Hailey's mom said, giving her a hug.

"We must go!" her dad cried.
"We don't want the parade to start
without us."

The hedgehogs took off, their wings glinting in the wintry sunshine. They flew fast, and soon they spotted Honeydew Meadow below them. A huge crowd of fairy animals was gathering there.

"Hurray!" cried Hailey. "We're not too late after all!"

Hailey, her mom and dad, and all their hedgehog friends fluttered to the ground and landed gently.

The Moss Mouse band was ready and waiting. Each mouse wore a lacy hat nibbled from a scarlet rosehip and, on their tails, a bow made from braided grass. They held their reed pipes and walnut shell drums ready to play. One tiny mouse started beating his drum eagerly as soon as he saw Hailey.

"Not yet, Morris," his mom whispered. "I'll tell you when to play."

"Hello, Moss Mice!" Hailey cried. "You all look so nice!" She could hardly wait for the music to begin.

Hailey's friend Bella the Bunny came hopping over. She was wearing a garland of white snowdrops around each long velvety ear and one around her neck. "Wow, you look fantastic, Hailey!" she cried.

"So do you," said Hailey.

She skipped around in a circle, too excited to keep still for even a moment.

Hailey heard some wings flapping above her head. She looked up eagerly and saw the Stardust Squirrels fluttering down. They were wearing garlands of polished nutshells and their fur shimmered with silver starlight. Hailey saw Sabrina and waved.

"Mom's Christmas cake looks

lovely—thanks to you," Sabrina called out to her.

Hailey grinned and puffed out her spikes proudly.

Next, the Cobweb Kittens arrived, their wings gleaming.

"Look at their costumes!" gasped Bella. The kittens wore garlands woven from glistening cobwebs and hung with bright, glimmering dewdrops.

"Everyone looks wonderful,"

Hailey said happily. "I'm so glad I got here in time."

Then the cheeky Pollen Puppies came scampering over, wagging their tails in excitement. "Whoo-hoo for the Christmas Parade!" they barked in chorus. "Whoo-hoo-woofy-whoo!"

Next, the Bark Badgers came marching past in a line, their silver wings neatly folded. Their black-and-white fur gleamed in the winter

sunshine, and they wore garlands made from beautifully carved bark shapes.

"And . . . halt!" cried the badger leader. They all stopped marching, and Hailey noticed Boris right at the back.

"Hi, Boris! How's your paw?" she called.

"Not too bad," he replied. "It won't stop me from being in the parade!"

103

Then the Holly Hamsters
arrived. Their golden fur shone
brightly, and around their necks
they wore garlands of crimson
holly berries.

Hugo came trotting over, grinning from ear to ear. "Just wait till everyone sees my holly bush," he whispered. "I bet they've never seen anything like it." His dark eyes widened suddenly. "Gosh," he said, stepping back and gazing at Hailey in astonishment. "You look beautiful, Hailey."

Hailey smiled. "Thanks, Hugo."

Finally, the Moonbeam Moles

appeared. They looked sleepy, but very happy to be there. Garlands of moonbeams hung around their necks, glowing like strings of pearls. Hailey looked over at Maisie and waved her paw. Maisie waved back with a snoozy smile.

Suddenly, the crowd fell silent. Hailey heard a gentle rustle from somewhere behind her. Turning, she saw an enormous bird flying toward Honeydew Meadow from

the Heart of Misty Wood. The
bird had huge feathery wings that
glinted gold in the sunshine. Her
brown eyes were big and round and
her beak was scarlet.

"Who's that?" asked Hugo
and Bella together, looking up in
wonder.

Hailey felt a great thrill of
excitement and her heart began
to thump. "I think . . . I think . . . it's
the Wise Wishing Owl!" she gasped.

CHAPTER SEVEN

The Leader of the Parade

The Wise Wishing Owl was so

beautiful that Hailey could do

nothing but stare as she glided

down into the meadow and folded
her vast wings. There was silence as
the fairy animals waited for her to
speak.

A smile spread slowly across
the owl's face. "Is everybody ready
for the Christmas Parade?" she
called at last. Her voice tinkled like
a waterfall splashing over rocks.

"Yes!" cried all the fairy
animals together. They looked at
one another in delight. The Wise

Wishing Owl, the oldest and most magical creature in Misty Wood, was hardly ever seen. This was a very special day indeed.

"Would you like to lead the parade, Your Wishingness?" asked one of the Bark Badgers.

The owl shook her feathery head. "Oh, no," she said. "One of you should take the lead. I have heard much of the Christmas Parade, and so I have come here to watch."

111

"Then will you do us the honor of *choosing* the leader for us?" asked the Bark Badger.

"Very well." The Wise Wishing Owl looked around at all the fairy animals, her snowy-white head turning slowly from side to side.

A shiver of delight ran through Hailey as the owl's gaze fell upon her. Never in her wildest dreams had she imagined that she would have the chance to look into the

deep brown eyes of the wonderful Wise Wishing Owl.

The owl furrowed her feathery brow. "It is not an easy choice," she said at last. "You all look very fine in your leaves and berries, your starshine and nutshells. But . . ." She stretched out a huge wing toward Hailey. "This little Hedgerow Hedgehog looks finer than anything I have ever seen. Will you lead the parade, my dear?"

Hailey gulped. She opened her mouth to reply, but no sound came out.

"Of course she will," squeaked

114

Bella, nodding at Hailey. "She would love to!"

Hailey took a deep breath. "Yes, I'd love to. Thank you, Wise Wishing Owl!" she cried.

"You are welcome," said the owl kindly.

"And you could start the parade off with your winter song, Hailey," Hugo piped up.

"Ooh, yes!" squealed Sabrina and Maisie.

All the fairy animals came crowding around. "We'd love to hear your song, Hailey," someone called out.

Hailey felt a tiny bit nervous, but she unfurled her wings and fluttered up above the other animals. Then she began to sing:

I love winter when the wild wind blows,

Scattering the leaves all around, all around,

Even though it chills my nose

and toes,

When I roll on the frosty ground.

As Hailey finished, her friends clapped and cheered. Hailey felt like she might burst with happiness. Then, chattering excitedly, all the fairy animals fluttered into line, ready for the Christmas Parade to begin.

The Hedgerow Hedgehogs scuttled to line up behind the

band. Behind them were the Bud Bunnies and the Cobweb Kittens. Then came the Holly Hamsters, the Moonbeam Moles, and the Stardust Squirrels. Behind the squirrels, the Bark Badgers marched into position. The Pollen Puppies were right at the back, yapping excitedly and running around in circles as they waited for everyone to begin moving.

"We're all ready!" cried Hailey

from high above. Light bounced off
her beautiful garland and sparkled
and danced all around Honeydew
Meadow.

The Moss Mouse band began
to play a marching song and
Hailey felt her toes twitching in
time to the music.

"I love winter!" she exclaimed
as she headed to the front of the
line. She was so happy that she did
a forward roll, picking up a few

fallen leaves on her prickles.

"And I *love* Christmas even more!"
she called as she uncurled again.
She looked back happily at all
her fairy animal friends, waiting
eagerly behind her for the parade
to start. "And this is the best
Christmas ever!"

Turn the page for lots of fun Misty Wood activities!

Connect the Dots

Follow the numbers and connect all the dots to make a lovely picture from the story. Start with dot number 1.

When you've finished connecting the dots, you can color the picture!

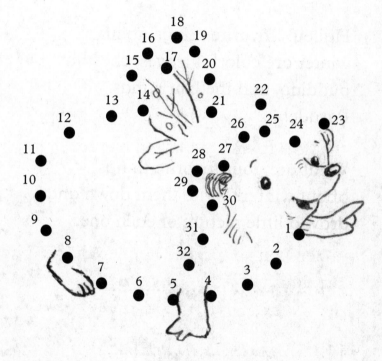

Winter Is Wonderful!

Hailey's favorite things about winter are colorful leaves, chestnut pudding, and the Christmas Parade!

What are your favorite things about winter? Write them down and draw a little picture of each one.

1. ....

2. ....

3. ....

Help Hugo Remember!

Hugo the Holly Hamster likes Hailey's song so much *he* wants to sing it, too! But Hugo can't remember all the words. Can you help him? Give it a try without looking back at the story!

I love winter when the wild ....
  blows,
Scattering the .... all around,
  all around,
Even though it chills my nose and
  ....,
When I roll on the frosty ....